"Where am I?"

Lord Crichton muttered upon regaining consciousness.

"You are in bed and you need not concern yourself," answered Deborah efficiently.

Turning a little, he caught a glimpse of a small, round window. "This," he said with certainty, "is *not* my bedchamber. What, pray, am I doing in *your* boudoir, madam?"

"This is *not* my boudoir," Deborah snapped.

Lord Crichton pondered this as his eyes came to rest on his coat over the chair. "What are you doing in *my* room, then?"

Deborah swallowed her indignation and tried for a composed and sensible speech. "I am accompanying you, my lord."

Beron gave a sudden heave and sat up in bed. "The question is, madam, to where?"

"To France, my lord."

Crichton closed his eyes. "I must have sustained a remarkable bump," he murmured. "I understood you to say I was on my way to France."

"I—I did."

The silence which followed was truly awful.

Books by Beth Bryan

HARLEQUIN REGENCY ROMANCE
50—WHAT LUCINDA LEARNED

A MANAGING FEMALE

BETH BRYAN

Harlequin Books

TORONTO • NEW YORK • LONDON
AMSTERDAM • PARIS • SYDNEY • HAMBURG
STOCKHOLM • ATHENS • TOKYO • MILAN

To Eilís and Aoileann,
who found the toad

Published December 1991

ISBN 0-373-31164-8

A MANAGING FEMALE

CHAPTER ONE

"Now Debs—" Peregrine Stormont's dark eyes twinkled as he regarded his elder sister "—you know this coach won't go any faster, no matter how you lean forward."

Miss Deborah Stormont started a little; then, meeting her brother's teasing glance, she smiled reluctantly and relaxed back against the squabs.

"You're right, Perry, but we were so out of reason delayed by that accident—"

Perry laughed. "What a lark! All those milk churns rolling about the road like skittles!"

"I'm glad you found it diverting." His sister glanced at him with some asperity. "But it has set us back two hours at the very least."

Perry gestured negligently towards the window. "We're bowling along nicely now."

"If only the boat may not have left without us!"

"Come, Debs! You don't think old Shaveley would hand us over to some shark who'd just take the ready and cut off without us, do you?"

"Nnnoo," Deborah conceded, thinking of that severe old gentleman, their man of business. "He's a high stickler, all right. But the captain may well be in haste. There is, I must suppose, the matter of the tide...."

"Well," said Peregrine with an air of great reasonableness, "if we miss this one, we shall have to catch another boat, that's all."

"But how shall we pay for it?" Deborah burst out, coming to the nub of the problem, as far as she was concerned. She clutched convulsively at the shabby portmanteau on the seat beside her. "We are almost at a stand as it is."

Perry grinned. "Then you'll have to pick a dandelion and polish off another of those sketches." He caught sight of his sister's face. "Oh, don't mind me, Debs. It's just my gibble-gabble. You know I'm not poking bogey at your drawing. You know I think it's just wonderful of you to be able to do it at all. And," he added admiringly, "as for your actually selling one to that Oxford beak—well, that's just top of the trees, that's all."

Deborah laughed. "I thank you, Perry."

"Not at all, not at all, and see here—" pleased at the result of his pacification technique, Perry determined to do the job thoroughly "—if we really do miss this wretched boat, then I'll lay my watch on the shelf, truly I will."

Miss Stormont paused a moment over this, then her brow cleared. "Oh, I see. I'm grateful to you, Perry, but I hope you won't have to pawn your watch."

"That's all right, then." Mr. Stormont leaned back and closed his eyes, apparently without a care in the world.

His sister smiled a trifle ruefully. If that wasn't just like Perry! Though, she had to admit, she did worry more than enough for two; not that she hadn't cause. She touched the small, worn bag again. She had never carried so much money before—yet it was even more unnerving that the sum represented all they had in the world. Again Deborah made the calculation in her head. No, it certainly wouldn't run to two more boat passages. There was barely enough for the inns on the other side, as it was.

She looked up at her brother. His chest gently rose and fell. Peregrine was taking a nap. Shaking her head, Deborah settled herself more comfortably. In one respect Peregrine was right: nothing she could do now would make them go faster. She must simply try to compose herself.

IF MISS STORMONT considered the pace on the Dover Road too slow, a traveller some ten miles farther ahead was beginning to feel he might perhaps be making too much speed.

Lord Auberon Crichton glanced expertly at the sun, then transferred the reins to one hand as he reached for his timepiece.

Just as he had thought, it was scarce past eleven. He knew he had started out too early. Even that accident between the farm carts hadn't held him up too greatly. Radwitch Hall was only thirty miles beyond Dover and he would be in that port within two hours; thus he would arrive at Radwitch in the afternoon, hours before dinner.

Lord Crichton's long, mobile mouth twitched. "What is this?" he murmured to himself. "Not getting cold feet, are you, my boy?"

The smile grew as he realized what he had said. It was absurd to consider a proposal to Gwen Phipps-Hedder an unpleasant task. He certainly wasn't being pushed into it. Why, only last month he had overheard his mother replying to a query on that very question.

"I expect," Lady Crichton had said tranquilly, "that Beron is perfectly able to make his own decisions." Her ladyship was a wise woman who perfectly understood that her son's gentle exterior hid a will of steel.

"Do you not think I should marry?" he had demanded later of his mother.

Lady Crichton laughed. "Yes, my dear, I think you should." She touched his cheek. "When you no longer care about *my* answer to such a question."

He thought she was being whimsical. But, oddly, her very lack of intensity led him to consider such a step more seriously. He had always assumed that he would marry, and now that he was approaching his thirtieth birthday, it seemed an appropriate time to act.

It was indeed ridiculous, he told himself, to talk of cold feet. It had been entirely his own decision. And it wasn't as if his offer would be in any way unwelcome if his recent interview with Sir Rodney Phipps-Hedder at his club in London was anything to go by.

"No, no, Crichton," Sir Rodney had declared, as his beefy fist smote Auberon's shoulder and Lord Crichton suppressed a wince. "Our house is your house, you know."

"Thank you, sir," he said.

"Not at all, not at all," Sir Rodney boomed. "Delighted to see you. Turn up round dinner time, have a drink, eat your vittles, take my young 'un for a turn about the rose garden, pop the question, come back in, break out the champagne and celebrate, what?"

"Quite so," murmured his lordship faintly, wondering if prolonged intercourse with Sir Rodney would permanently damage his hearing. "I apprehend Miss Phipps-Hedder has no objection to receiving an offer from me?"

Sir Rodney laughed—a sound louder, if possible, than his speaking voice. "Ha! Ha! You will have your little joke, my lord. But Gwen's a good girl."

"I don't doubt it," Lord Crichton replied. Then a touch of steel entered his soft tones. "However, I do not desire a wife who weds me merely at her father's bidding."

"Ha! Ha!" Sir Rodney's laughter shook the walls of his town house, and it was all Crichton could do not to clap his hands over his ears. Sir Rodney waved a fat finger in his face. "Don't be selling yourself short, my lord. What gel

wouldn't want to marry you, eh? Fortune, title, looks..."
He nudged Crichton with a well-padded elbow. "What
more could a gel want, what?" He chuckled, and his native shrewdness reasserted itself. "You're not doing so
badly yourself, my lord. We're an old family, too, and my
girl's not coming to you empty-handed." He wielded his
elbow again.

Moving unobtrusively backwards, Lord Crichton hoped
he might escape this interview without a cracked rib. He
stood up. "I thank you for your hospitality, sir. I shall be
with you and Lady Phipps-Hedder in two days' time,
then."

"Ah, yes!" Sir Rodney heaved his bulk out of his armchair and stood looking at his guest, huffing a little. It
seemed impossible for his ruddy face to become any red-
der, but it suddenly came to Lord Crichton that his host
was embarrassed.

"Is there something else we should discuss, sir?" he
asked encouragingly.

Sir Rodney blew out his breath so that the ends of his
grey military moustache quivered. "Gels will be gels, eh,
my lord? No harm in it, no harm at all."

"None in the world," agreed his puzzled, but polite,
guest.

"I don't hold with schooling for females," Sir Rodney
suddenly declared. "A gel belongs at home till she's married and then off to her own place."

"But I understood that Miss Phipps-Hedder had attended the Athenian Academy—"

"Hummph!" The volume of Sir Rodney's snort set the
china ornaments on the mantelpiece rattling. He studied
the carpet. Then, in his lowest tones yet, he added, "My
wife, you know."

There was a silence, during which both gentlemen contemplated the Aubusson in silent tribute to Lady Phipps-Hedder's influence.

"Met someone there," Sir Rodney went on at last. "French girl—good family, though," he went on hastily. "I looked into that thoroughly. I wasn't going to have my girl on the jaunter with some jumped-up froggies no one's ever heard of."

Lord Crichton looked at his host and wondered how the gentle and shy Miss Phipps-Hedder had ever sprung from such a sire.

"But these de Keroualles—they're the old stock, all right. Lost all their money in the Revolution, of course, but of the old aristocracy."

"Quite so," Lord Crichton interposed, hoping to bring his prospective father-in-law to the point. "So you deemed them suitable companions for your daughter?"

"Just so. Now the point is this, my lord. My girl's wanted to visit this French mam'zelle. But the family were émigrés, of course and they went back to France just before this Boney fellow started up again. So of course there was no question of a visit until Wellington had put paid to this Corsican upstart."

"Naturally not," agreed Lord Crichton, stifling a yawn.

"But now, they tell me, it's all right. I went to the Foreign Office just last week and the Secretary himself told me he wouldn't hesitate to let his own daughter go on such a trip."

"Ah! So Miss Phipps-Hedder plans a trip to France?"

"You're quick, my lord, there's no denying it. Aye, that's the matter in a nutshell. Provided you've no objection, of course."

"I?" Lord Crichton's eyebrows rose. "It is surely a matter between you and your daughter, sir."

"Aye, aye, but she'll be your responsibility soon enough."

Deftly, Lord Crichton dodged another ferocious dig in the ribs. "When does Miss Phipps-Hedder leave, then?"

"Four days. I'll send a footman and her maid with her, of course, and the Frenchies will meet her on the other side, so there's no cause for concern."

"And she will return?"

"About a month, say early September. Lady Phipps-Hedder thinks you might care to visit us again then, and if you agree, the engagement could be announced when you come back to us at Christmas."

"Lady Phipps-Hedder's arrangements are always admirable." Crichton bowed and made his escape.

The din of a London street, he reflected, had been a blessed relief after his host's roar. Even now, he thought, looking ahead along the Dover Road, his ears tingled at the prospect of another conversational bout with Sir Rodney.

He lurched in the saddle and looked quickly down at his mount. The gait of the powerful grey had altered. Immediately he brought the horse to a halt at the side of the road and slid off. He ran his hands over the flanks, then lifted the legs. At one of the rear hooves, he made a small sound of annoyance. The grey had shed a shoe.

Lord Crichton stood back and studied his horse. The big grey was happily chomping on a patch of sweet clover. "It's well for you," Crichton told him, "you can walk but I may not ride." He gathered the reins and urged the horse forward. "It's Shanks' mare for me, unless some kind person takes pity on me."

"ARE WE THERE YET?" Perry Stormont sat up and looked at his sister with the clear, untroubled gaze of an awakening child.

"Not yet." Deborah consulted an old-fashioned watch-brooch. "But we should certainly be there within the hour."

"Lord," Perry yawned prodigiously and stretched. "How flat this journey has been! Why, those milk churns were the most exciting thing that has happened the whole time!"

"Were you expecting highwaymen?" Deborah smiled at him, thinking that, although he had just turned twenty, there was still a lot of the boy in Perry.

"Dick Turpin? No, that would be too much to ask for."

"What, then?"

"Oh, I don't know. Anything out of the ordinary." He pushed his head out of the window. Muffled, his voice came back to her. "By George, Debs, take a look at that piece of horseflesh."

"Perry, do be careful!"

"Take a look, Debs. There, by the side of the road. Look at those shoulders and the hocks!"

Deborah risked a quick glance. "But why is it walking on the verge? Can it be injured?"

"You must be right, Debs. Dashed bad luck for a prime goer like that and for the rider, too, of course." He poked his head out again.

Deborah leaned forward to catch his words.

"Yes, cast a shoe, I shouldn't wonder. He won't want to risk riding him any farther."

The coach came closer and Peregrine hung dangerously out. "I say, Debs—" his voice floated back to her "—he looks a gentleman. Let's take him up with us."

Deborah looked alarmed. "But, Perry, we don't know—"

But she was too late. Perry had leaned back inside and tugged energetically at the check-string. The coach had scarcely stopped when he flung the door open and leapt out.

Deborah sighed. Then she quickly patted her thick dark hair into place and tried to shake some of the wrinkles out of her gown. However, she thought bleakly, no amount of shaking would alter its drab colour or old-fashioned cut. But, she vowed, lifting her chin, she would not be ashamed of honest poverty. She folded her long, elegant hands in her lap and suppressing an unladylike urge to peer out the open door, she sat back to await the arrival of her brother and the stranger.

"Debs." Awe and excitement battled in Perry's voice. "Debs, here is Lord Crichton."

Deborah looked up at the man in the doorway. He was tall, but rather slightly built, she thought, until she saw that his shoulders filled the opening. Sunlight caught auburn glints in his dark hair, but his face was in shadow.

"Miss Stormont?" His voice was pleasantly low-pitched. He bowed over her hand, despite the cramped quarters. "I am most grateful for your kindness in rescuing this unhappy traveller."

"We are happy to be of assistance, sir," Deborah said in a rush, unaccountably flustered. "But will you not be seated?"

"Thank you." He sat down opposite her. Calling to the coachman, Perry scrambled into his place beside him.

"What a sweet goer that is, sir," he said in his impetuous way. "A regular sixteen-mile-an-hour tit, I'll wager. Tell me I am right!"

The stranger smiled and Deborah realized it was a charming smile, lighting those grey eyes and lessening the rather aloof effect of the straight nose and high cheekbones.

"He was sired by Great Sultan."

"Great Sultan—do you mean the Derby winner . . ."

"I should be delighted to discuss all this with you," Lord Crichton said in his gentle way, "but I fear to bore Miss Stormont with such talk."

"Debs?" Peregrine stared. "She won't mind!"

Lord Crichton's grey eyes met Miss Stormont's black ones. A smile quirked at the corner of his generous mouth and Deborah saw that the irony of his glance had been warmed by sympathy. It was an expression she had had little experience of recently, and somehow it made her more uncertain than ever. "Pray don't mention it," she gasped, "no, no, not at all—" She broke off, thinking angrily that she was babbling.

Lord Crichton remained oblivious to any lack of finesse in her remarks. "You are too kind," he said, "but I should feel most guilty if I repaid your kindness with a monologue on the breeding of cattle."

His even tones had not changed, but Deborah was surprised to note that Peregrine accepted his refusal without demur. She looked at Lord Crichton with renewed interest.

"Your brother tells me you are bound for France," he remarked politely.

"Yes," Deborah said. Then, flushing a little at the baldness of her response, she went on hurriedly, "We are visiting an aunt of ours who lives there."

"And do you make a long stay in that country?" Lord Crichton directed his attention to Peregrine.

Perry laughed. "Ask Debs," he said. "She makes all those decisions."

To her annoyance, Deborah found herself reddening again. "Really, Perry! You make me sound like an archwife or at the very least an odiously managing female."

Peregrine grinned unrepentantly. "Well, you manage me, don't you? Not that I'm complaining, mind. I haven't the head for all these details." He caught his sister's eye and threw up his hands in a gesture of surrender, then turned quickly to their guest. "Are you planning a sea voyage too, sir?"

"No, I am to visit friends to the north of Dover. Is this your first trip to France, Miss Stormont?" Lord Crichton spoke courteously to Deborah.

"First trip anywhere," put in the irrepressible Peregrine. "Never been out of Salisbury before in our lives!"

"Salisbury?" Smoothly, Lord Crichton picked up his cue. "That is a most interesting part of the country. The antiquities, now..."

The conversation ran on in rather conventional tracks. Deborah made correct remarks on Stonehenge, Avebury, the Cathedral and other points of note, but she gave her complete attention to a covert study of their new acquaintance.

There could be no doubt he was a gentleman; every detail of his person, from the carefully tended hands to the poise of his head proclaimed that fact. And the clothes! Deborah had never seen a coat so well fitted. It seemed almost glued to his shoulders. How had he managed to get into it at all, she wondered. And his breeches! The like of them had certainly never been seen in Salisbury. The buckskin clung to those muscular calves as if they, too, had been painted there. But the final touch was the boots. He had been riding since early morning, but the dust of the highway seemed to have dimmed their lustre not at all. Deborah had heard that some Town smarts actually used champagne to polish their boots. Looking at those glistening surfaces, she could well believe it. No wonder Perry was overwhelmed by this pattern-card of masculine perfection.

Lord Crichton, of course, was not unaware of Deborah's scrutiny. He was, if anything, rather amused by it. Miss Stormont had quite a schoolmarmish air, and he was entertained that she should find him an object of such concentration. He maintained his demeanor of well-bred attention and, far more subtly, made his own study of Miss Stormont.

She was, he realized, younger than he had at first thought. He had been misled by her self-possessed manner, her dark unfashionable dress and severe hairstyle. But on a closer look, he saw that her hair was long and glossy, a real ebony. And he knew several reigning beauties who would have given their eye-teeth for skin like hers, white as a magnolia petal. Her eyes, too, were a real black with astonishingly long lashes. Fair beauties were in fashion, but if Miss Stormont came to Town, he had no doubt that she could cut quite a dash—that is, if she acquired a whole new wardrobe and lost all that starch.

She and her brother were orphans, he gathered. The girl had had to take responsibility too young. Hard on her of course, but, as for himself, he had always disliked managing women.... Crichton became aware that he had been asked a question.

"Yes," he said, glancing hastily out the window, "we are coming into Dover now."

Deborah consulted her watch again. "I hope we shan't be late."

"Tell me, my lord," Peregrine demanded, "do you know when the boats leave for Cherbourg?"

Crichton looked slightly surprised. "I do not know, I'm afraid. It is many years since I made the crossing, but I should suppose that they depend on the tides." He looked from brother to sister. "But surely you told me your passage was already arranged?"

"Yes, our man of business arranged it."

Lord Crichton's eyes rested on Deborah who was biting her lip. "Then surely you need not trouble yourselves."

What a ninnyhammer she must look, dithering about before this sophisticated beau. He must think her a real bumpkin. "We were delayed by an accident on the road, my lord, so I'm naturally rather anxious."

"Poor old Debs." Perry clapped her rather boisterously on the shoulder. "Hate to have things out of your own hands, don't you?"

Deborah stared stonily at Perry for a moment, then, mastering her annoyance, she said, "Where may we leave you, Lord Crichton?"

"Anywhere, Miss Stormont. I shall take my horse to a farrier and hope to resume my journey later this afternoon."

"Pray let us know when it is convenient for you then, sir."

"We are entering an area of many inns. I should easily find what I need here."

"Very well. Pull the check-string, Perry, please."

The coach swayed to a stop and Crichton prepared to disembark. But as he took Miss Stormont's hand, a feeling of compunction struck him. Peregrine Stormont was clearly an amiable rattle, but scarcely a source of real support. There should, of course, have been a duenna or maid of some sort. But he supposed the funds wouldn't run to that. The coach was clearly hired.

He looked at Miss Stormont. She was obviously worried, and though not a schoolroom miss, she was young and inexperienced. They had been kind to him and it would be no very fair recompense if he now abandoned them. And after all, he told himself, he did have several hours to spare.

"Miss Stormont," he said, "will you permit me to offer you some recompense for your helpfulness to me? I know you have never been to Dover before and the quays can be confusing. I have some slight familiarity with them and should be glad to assist you as best I may. If you agree, I shall quickly leave my horse with a smith and return to you."

A wave of relief swept over Deborah. She had felt sadly out of her depth since leaving Salisbury, and Perry, of course, could not be expected to share her concerns. But before she could speak, Peregrine burst out, "What a capital idea, my lord. I'll help you untie the horse and find the smith." He bounded down and vanished.

Lord Crichton smiled. "I hope my plan is as welcome to you, Miss Stormont?"

"Oh, yes." Deborah smiled up at him. "I own I shall be most grateful for your assistance."

She looked quite five years younger and far more attractive when she smiled, Crichton thought as he led the horse off. It really was a pity she was such a starched-up female.

CHAPTER TWO

THEY HAD STOPPED at a small coaching inn, and while she waited, Deborah sat in the small, sheltered garden, sipping tea. She was surprised to find that the burning anxiety she had felt earlier had dissipated. She was still rather uneasy, but she was not nearly so close to panic. Not that Lord Crichton had exactly entered into her own concern, but there was no denying his calm confidence was reassuring.

So it was true, she thought with a smile: a worry shared was a worry halved. Well, Perry had better watch out! She just might demand more of him in the future. She smiled again and her thoughts went back to Lord Crichton. It must be wonderful to go through life in such a way—to greet every occurrence with such light, amused irony, knowing that nothing had the power to disturb one's secure, ordered life....

"Here we are again, Debs." Peregrine stood at the gate. "We've left the horse and the coach is waiting. Let's be on our way."

"What is the name of the ship you are to travel on, Miss Stormont?" his lordship enquired as they rumbled off again.

"The *Orient Wave*," she answered promptly, "and the captain is Captain MacKenzie."

"Ah, good. That should make it easy to find."

"Find?" Deborah blinked at him. Insofar as she had considered the matter, she had imagined the port as a species of marine coaching station, with the boats in a kind of line.

"Why, yes." He smiled at her. "There is more than one boat bound for the French coast, you know."

When they arrived at the port, Deborah saw that this was an understatement. Dozens of boats of all shapes and sizes floated on the dark green water. Half the population of England seemed to be here, carrying bags, hoisting bales and barrels, winding ropes, rushing about on unknown errands, calling loudly back and forth to one another, all of them completely indifferent to the new arrivals.

"I must enquire as to the *Orient Wave*," Lord Crichton said. "Will you wait for me?" He pointed to a small shed at the end of a nearby pier. "You will be safely out of the way there."

Deborah watched as a great square bale swung overhead. "What can that be?"

"Wool for the Low Countries, I should expect, Miss Stormont. I shall be back with you as soon as I may." He plunged through a crowd unloading a long cart and was lost to view in the mêlée.

"Come on, then." Peregrine took her arm and they made their way over to the shed as the porter trundled their luggage behind them in something very like a common wheelbarrow.

With their backs against the wooden walls, the Stormonts looked with bright eyes at the scene before them.

"Where can all these people come from, Perry?"

"Never seen such a crush. It's better than the square at home on market day." Perry turned his head from side to side. "Look out there!" he cried. "I say, did you see that, Debs? That chap was nearly beaned by that barrel."

"There seem to be winches and cranes everywhere. It will be a miracle if someone is not hurt."

"Right. The *Orient Wave* is at anchor, just down this way." Lord Crichton had returned. He took the Stormonts by the arm. "It would appear you had good grounds for your anxiety, Miss Stormont. The tide is on the turn, they tell me, but the *Orient Wave* has not yet lifted anchor; however, we should not keep the good captain waiting any longer." Deftly he guided them through the tangle of ropes, carts and goods.

"Ah, this should be it!" He stopped by one of the longer piers. "There!" He pointed to a large, red-painted boat, riding at anchor halfway down the pier. "There's the *Orient Wave*."

As they followed his gesture, the Stormonts saw another luggage cart being trundled up the gangway. There was another passenger, then, or even more than one, if the mound of luggage meant anything.

At Lord Crichton's words, a compact, burly man with a sailor's gait and captain's cap turned to them. "Your pardon, sir," he said with a rich Scottish burr, "would ye be Mr. Stormont, then?" He rolled the *R*s fearsomely.

"This is Mr. Stormont here and his sister, Miss Stormont."

"Have we delayed you, Captain?" Deborah asked.

"No, no. Dinna fash yerself, Miss Stormont. But I'm intending to sail with the ebb and I'll be glad tae see all my passengers safely stowed."

"Then it is time for us to say goodbye, Miss Stormont." Lord Crichton bowed over her hand. "I shall be forever grateful for your kindness." He straightened up.

"Look out there, man!" Captain MacKenzie shouted.

"Your head, sir! Your head!" Peregrine cried and made a dive towards his lordship. But he was too late. A wooden crate, dipping dangerously low, had swung past, and just as Lord Crichton rose from his bow, a corner of it struck his head and knocked him senseless to the ground.

Immediately Deborah fell to her knees beside him. She felt in the thick black hair. "There is no cut, but the lump is large," she said, reaching for his lordship's pulse.

"Will he be all right?" Peregrine asked. He was pale, for like many robust young men, he had a horror of sickness and injury.

"I should think so." Deborah held his wrist. "His pulse is strong."

"He canna lie here," put in the captain.

"Of course not." Deborah slipped off her spencer and folded it into a pillow for his head. "Perhaps an inn..."

"Forby!" Captain MacKenzie snorted a little. "I'm nae one tae abandon a man in his need, but the tide willnae wait for us. Has he nae servant to take charge of him and take him to an inn back in the town?"

"We haven't seen one," Peregrine said doubtfully.

"What's tae be done, then?"

"We certainly can't leave him here." Deborah stood up and dusted her hands, frowning. "I believe it to be a simple concussion, but such head injuries may be deceptive. He must be closely watched and kept quiet, even after he wakes."

"What's to do then, Debs?" Perry repeated the captain's query.

Deborah stared over the crowded quays. The accident had caused little stir, though a small knot of curious bystanders had come to gawk. None of them offered assistance or advice. Biting her lip, Deborah looked round.

Back where the quays began there had been a smattering of rather dilapidated inns and taverns. She could not feel they inspired confidence as sanctuary for an injured man. Nor, she concluded, running her eyes over the crowd, did anyone there look particularly reliable.

Lord Crichton had spoken of visiting friends ... to the north of Dover, wasn't it? But he had not mentioned any names. Besides, she thought as she glanced down at the shabby portmanteau by her feet, she certainly did not possess enough money to pay for his conveyance to his friends, or indeed for his care here.

Captain MacKenzie's voice roused her from her thoughts. He was calling up to his crew. She could see them busily battening down the cargo holds, so the *Orient Wave* must be ready to cast off.

"We have only one choice," she said decisively. "We must bring him abroad."

"To France!" Peregrine gaped at her.

"Well, I own it is not the ideal solution. But what else can we do? If we take him to an inn ourselves, we miss the boat and tide. And—" her eyes swept over the onlookers again "—I hope you don't think we should entrust him to any of these villains."

"Wouldn't say they're villains exactly, Debs," Perry demurred, "but I agree I wouldn't want 'em looking after me."

"Captain MacKenzie," Deborah called, "will you summon some men to carry his lordship aboard?"

Frowning, the captain returned, "Bring him wi'us, you mean?"

"Yes, do you object?"

The captain shrugged. "He's your friend and your responsibility and it's my responsibility tae take that tide, for I've cargo as well as passengers tae think on. But Miss Stormont, where am I tae put him?" The captain looked at her under bushy brows.

"Put him?"

"I've my full complement of passengers now. I've nae room for anither."

"He can share my cabin, surely?" put in Peregrine. "I'll gladly sleep on the floor."

"Aye, if you're willing, I've naught against that. And there's twa bunks in each cabin, so you'll nae put yerself oot."

"Let us move him, then," Deborah said rather impatiently. "He should be in bed." She stepped back and watched as the captain summoned two sailors. Then she followed as they carried Lord Crichton aboard the *Orient Wave.*

In Perry's cabin, the crewmen laid Crichton gently on the lower bed. She thanked them, pressed a small coin in each palm, then asked them to show Perry where he might find a basin of cool water and some clean cloths. Tipping their fingers to their foreheads, they took Perry off with them.

Debs turned her attention to her patient. With some effort she drew his boots off and placed them reverently beside the bunk. She fumbled about, trying to loosen his cravat, then realized it was held by a pin. Her eyes widened at the size of the twisted gold head, hidden in the intricate folds. She rolled the cravat carefully and stuck the pin through it, lest the valuable trinket be lost. Now she could loosen the shirt about his neck. The fineness of the linen amazed her; only in some old things in Mama's trunk had she ever seen cloth so fine.

She covered him with the sheet, then sat down to await Perry's return. Meanwhile, she studied Lord Crichton, her fingers resting gently on his wrist, monitoring his pulse. His face was pale, but he breathed as easily and as calmly as if he slept. His dark lashes lay upon his cheeks and his generous mouth was relaxed in repose. She could see no trace of the ironic smile that seemed almost constant in waking.

It was an attractive face, Debs thought, and her gaze went to his hands. He wore no rings at all, but of course that proved nothing. It would be surprising, though, if such a nobleman were unmarried. She wondered if they ought to make some effort to reach his wife and family... but how...

"Back at last." Peregrine struggled through the narrow doorway. He carried a tin tray with an enamelled basin and a stack of clean if rather roughly woven cloths.

"Good." Deborah placed the tray on the little bedside table, then rummaged in the reticule hanging from her wrist and produced a small vial. She shook a few drops into the water and the scent of roses filled the room.

"Lord, Debs," said Perry, wrinkling his nose, "the poor man will smell like an opera dancer's boudoir."

His sister looked up from wringing out a cloth. "And what, pray," she asked with a twinkle in her black eyes, "do you know of boudoirs, opera dancer's or otherwise?"

Perry grinned. "Common knowledge, my dear, common knowledge, don't you know?"

"I don't! But I do know that rose oil is refreshing and soothing. I expect Lord Crichton will have a most shocking headache when he awakes."

"If he don't, he will have when he realizes he's been kidnapped off to France."

"Perry! How can you say such a thing. Of course we haven't kidnapped his lordship."

"We haven't exactly asked his permission, either."

At this point Lord Crichton moaned and turned his head. Deborah instantly shifted his pillow slightly and

placed the damp cloth on his forehead. His lordship made
no other move.

"Look, Debs," Perry began, "Captain MacKenzie says
he'll be casting off in twenty minutes. I'd love to see it. You
go off to your cabin. It's just down the corridor there, and
your key's in the door. Brush your hair or whatever it is
females do to freshen themselves and I'll watch his lordship till you come back."

"Very well." Deborah looked once more at her patient.
"Change the cloths as they dry and send someone for me
instantly if there's any change."

She easily found the cabin and discovered her meagre
baggage already in place. She was glad to sink down onto
a stool. In front of her was a small table and over it a scrap
of mirror. Debs gasped as she peered at herself. Her hair
hung in straggles at each side of her face and there were
dark shadows under her eyes, which themselves looked
huge in her pale face.

This will never do, she thought, reaching for her dressing box. She brushed her hair, then pinned it back in a tidy
but rather severe roll. There was water in the ewer, so she
poured some into the small basin and splashed her face.

That brought a little colour into her cheeks, but there
was not a great deal she could do about those shadows.
Still, she shook out her cuffs and smoothed down her col-
lar. She reached into a bag, pulled out a shawl, and drap-
ing it over her shoulders she went back to Perry.

Lord Crichton's condition had not changed, so she dismissed her brother and placed a fresh compress on the patient's brow. Her long, delicate fingers brushed away the
straight black hair, her butterfly touch soothing the faint
lines between his fine brows.

There was a sudden change in the movement of the boat,
and Deborah felt that rise of excitement all travellers ex-

perience when their journey has truly begun. But she kept her attention on Lord Crichton, a tiny frown beginning to form between her own brows.

Now that her decision was irrevocable, she was beginning to have second thoughts. What if his lordship were seriously injured? She doubted that Captain MacKenzie carried a medical officer. Had she perhaps been a trifle precipitate in deciding? She looked uneasily at the still form. What would he say when he found himself on the high seas and not the Dover Road?

"Debs! You must come right away! You mustn't miss this!" Perry burst in. He tried to moderate his voice but his excitement was obvious.

"Hush, Perry, whatever is the matter?"

"Sorry, Debs." Perry glanced at the bunk, and then, in an exaggerated whisper, he went on, "It's the cliffs. Debs, we're in open water now and the view! Captain Mac-Kenzie says you should not miss such a famous sight."

"But what about—"

"Oh, I'll look after his lordship. Do go up! You cannot imagine what it is—"

"Oh, I should like to see it, all right." Deborah took Lord Crichton's wrist once more. "His lordship is as before, but be sure you send for me if anything changes." She pulled her shawl tighter and went out.

Up on the deck, the wind blew freshly and she breathed deeply. It was pleasant to be out of the tiny cabin. She walked over to the rails and was surprised to see how far they had come. Duty had apparently called Captain MacKenzie elsewhere, though she could see several crewmen busy about their tasks.

She looked out across the glinting water. The white cliffs gleamed like snow, capped by the green velvet meadows.

Below, the deeper green waves broke in white froth at their base. She gazed, enchanted.

"Lifts the jolly old heart, eh?"

Deborah jumped and whirled round.

"Oh, I say! Steady on, ma'am. Didn't mean to startle you."

She smiled a trifle uncertainly at the newcomer. He was a young man, though slightly older, she guessed, than Perry. His mop of bright red curls and round freckled face gave him an air of ingenuousness at odds with his dandified clothing. "Forgive me," she said, "I did not hear you approaching."

"Remiss of me." The young man inclined his head. "Forgive me and permit me to introduce myself. . . fellow passengers and all that, eh?"

Debs was feeling foolish at her startled reaction, so she smiled reassuringly at him. "There can be no impropriety in such an introduction, sir."

He bowed elaborately. "Frederick Wimpole at your service, ma'am."

"And I am Deborah Stormont, Mr. Wimpole."

"Call me Freddie. Everybody does. We travellers have to stick together, what? Do you speak French, Miss Stormont?"

"Some," Deborah admitted. "But I have had little opportunity for practice and it is many years since my lessons."

"Practice don't seem to make any difference to me," the young man said gloomily. "Just can't seem to get my tongue around those Frenchie words. Mind you—" he brightened "—I find I can say 'doo van' and they'll bring me some dashed decent wine."

"Then you are managing very well," Deborah said gravely. "Do you go to France often, Mr. Wi—I mean, Freddie?"

Mr. Wimpole sank into gloom again. "I do, that is to say, since Boney was *romped* and my aunt went back there."

"Ah, I also am visiting an aunt myself."

"Well, I hope she's not such an old Tough as mine." Freddie sighed, and placing his elbows on the rail, he dropped his chin in his hands.

Deborah was a little at a loss as to respond to this confidence. "I'm sure your aunt must be delighted to see you."

"She don't act like it."

"Some old ladies can be very difficult," Deborah ventured.

Freddie shook his head. "Rather fancy this one's in a class of her own." He looked at Debs. "Always dying, you know."

"Dying?"

"Sends me a message: 'Sinking fast, come at once.' And when I get there, I find she's fitter than a regiment of Horse Guards. Probably outlive them all, too." He sighed again, dolefully.

"Well, you are to be congratulated on your sense of familial responsibility," Deborah tried to hearten him. She stepped away from the rails. "But I am afraid that I must go below now."

Freddie pulled himself upright and bowed again. "Delighted to have met you, Miss Stormont. We'll meet again at dinner, no doubt."

"Good afternoon, sir." Just before she went down, Deborah turned for one last look at the coast, receding rapidly into the afternoon haze.

For a moment, she had a sudden presentiment: leaving England was to be a turning point in her life and nothing would ever be quite the same for her again. She was not normally given to such fantastical thoughts. She shook her head rather impatiently and went downstairs to see how his lordship fared.

CHAPTER THREE

LORD CRICHTON was swimming under water, deep water. He fought his way upwards, his head and lungs bursting and, as his head broke through the waves, he opened his eyes.

"It's all right, my lord, you will be better directly," a brisk but pleasant voice reassured him and cool hands touched his forehead.

"Where am I?" Lord Crichton muttered; a part of his mind reflected that this was scarcely an original response.

"You are in bed and you need not concern yourself," the voice replied, but this time it sounded slightly less assured.

The room was dimly lit, but Lord Crichton could see boards above his head, and by turning a little, he caught a glimpse of a small, round window. "This," he said with certainty, "is not my bedchamber." He sniffed and looked towards the voice again. "What am I doing in your boudoir, madam?"

"This is not my boudoir!" the voice answered indignantly.

Lord Crichton pondered this as he squinted in the same direction. That was definitely a feminine silhouette, and equally definitely, that was his coat over the chair. "What are you doing in *my* room, then?"

She had been fiddling with an oil lamp. Now she turned the key and the cabin brightened. "You have had a knock on the head, my lord. You were taken here to recover."

Beron gave a sudden heave and sat up in bed. "The question is, madam, where is 'here'?"

"Pray be careful," Deborah cried. "You must not hit your head again!"

"No," agreed Crichton, cautiously sitting back against the bunk head. "It already feels as though some incompetent carpenter were sawing away at the back of my brain. Who hit me?"

"No one, my lord. You were caught by the edge of a bale being lifted aboard."

"I know you," Crichton declared suddenly. "You're the woman from the carriage. St-Sto-Stormont—that's it, Miss Stormont!"

"That is correct, my lord."

"But you were on your way to France."

There was no way to evade the matter, Deborah thought. She clenched her hands tighter. "So are you, my lord."

Crichton closed his eyes. "I must have sustained a remarkable bump," he murmured. "I understood you to say that I was on my way to France."

"I—I did."

There was a silence. Then his lordship sat up straighter. "I fear my wits are not at their best, Miss Stormont. My recollection is that I was bound for Radwitch Hall, which is, I should suppose, still situated near Tillsborough?"

"I should suppose." Deborah did not look at him.

"And yet," he went on meditatively, "this is undoubtedly a cabin and I am aware of motion and you tell me I am en route to France. Pray enlighten me, Miss Stormont." The soft tones did not vary, but there was an implacable note in them.

Deborah gripped her hands more tightly and forced herself to meet those ironic grey eyes. "You were rendered unconscious, my lord. I knew of no responsible person to whom I might consign your care, and Captain MacKenzie was anxious not to miss the tide. Neither my brother nor I could convey you to some respectable establishment without losing passage on the *Orient Wave*. I could perceive no alternative to having you brought aboard."

His lordship closed his eyes. "A managing woman. I knew it from the moment I set eyes on you."

Deborah opened her mouth and then closed it. His lordship was pale and there was a strained look about his wide mouth. And, after all, he had cause to be a trifle mifty. "I have some laudanum drops with me, my lord. If you will consent to swallow some, I believe you will do better after a sleep."

"If it will silence this infernal carpenter, I'll swallow anything."

Deborah handed him the glass. Then she fluffed up the pillow, and as he sank down again, he felt the cool, feathery touch of those long white hands. *Beautiful hands,* he thought, *beautiful hands,* even if the owner was a dashed governessy take-charge.

WHEN HE AWOKE AGAIN, his head was clear and Peregrine was sitting in the chair by his bunk.

"What time is it?" he demanded.

"Just after seven," Peregrine said helpfully. "How do you go on, my lord?"

Crichton moved his head. "The carpenter has mercifully ceased," he said.

Perry looked puzzled. "Carpenter?"

"I am better, but I see that this trip to France is no dream."

"Well," said Peregrine magnanimously, "I told Debs you'd be entitled to kick up a dust, but I assure you, my lord, we were in a devil of a coil."

And you've placed me in an equally devilish one, his lordship thought, but did not say so. Just the thought of Sir Rodney made his head ache. He reached for his boots.

"I say!" Peregrine was alarmed. "Do you think you should, my lord? I mean, are you steady enough on your pins? Debs said you should be quiet—"

"My legs will do." His lordship stood up, staggered and put his hand on the upper bunk to steady himself. He saw Perry's night things tossed carelessly up there. "But I assure you, another five minutes in this pokey little cabin will take me to the Gates of Bedlam and Miss Stormont cannot prescribe that."

"No, but, my lord... Pray be careful! Perhaps I should call m'sister—"

"Mr. Stormont, I gather that we are to share these very confined quarters. If we are to conduct ourselves with any degree of civility, I beg you will cease 'my lording' me every minute. You may call me Beron. What is your name?"

"Perry—Peregrine."

"Very well, then, Peregrine. You may give me your arm and help me up those stairs. I trust that there is somewhere on this wretched tub where one may take the air?"

Perry grinned. "There's a sheltered little deck for passengers just up here."

"Lead me to it."

Once out in the air, Perry checked. The deck was not empty. A long wooden chair had been set out and a redheaded young man, with a rug wrapped loosely about his legs, reclined there.

Lord Crichton stopped and groaned. "Freddie! I thought this was a dream. Now I see it is rapidly becoming a nightmare."

"Beron!" The young man gaped. Then, as his lordship's words sank in, he sat up and blinked indignantly at him. "What do you mean, 'nightmare'?"

Perry was setting out chairs for Lord Crichton and himself. Beron touched him on the arm as he thanked him. "Peregrine, may I introduce Frederick Wimpole? He is a harmless creature, but subject to delusions. For instance, he is of the opinion that the object he is wearing is a waistcoat."

"It looks splendid to me." Perry gazed with unfeigned admiration at the cream and crimson stripes.

Freddie threw him a grateful glance. "I should think so! Paddington's just introduced 'em. Soon they'll be all the crack."

"My poor boy, this is only to be expected if you insist upon patronizing a coaching station rather than a tailor."

"Doing it too brown, Beron. Why, Paddington's already sold several to Prinny himself."

"That alone should have warned you, Freddie."

Mr. Wimpole grinned. "Shan't expect to see you in one, then, Beron?"

Lord Crichton stretched himself the length of the long wooden chair. "I shall shut my eyes, Freddie, and hope you will have the decency to cover yourself."

"Here!" Mr. Wimpole forgot his waistcoat. "Here, Beron! What are you doin' here? Thought you were goin' to Radwitch with old Huff-and-Gruff, though I can't for the life of me see why—"

"Frederick, I beg leave to inform you that you are referring to my future father-in-law."

"Whaaat?" Freddie stared, his eyes rounder than ever. He had gone quite pale and had apparently sustained a shock.

Beron looked rather quizzically at him. "Come, Freddie, I should have thought they were making wagers on it in the clubs. My offer for Gwendolyn Phipps-Hedder can scarcely come as a surprise to the ton."

"Ah!" Freddie had recovered. "Gwendolyn. Just so. Caught me off balance there for a moment, old chap, but let me be the first to congratulate you." Freddie's enthusiasm grew. "Dashed good news! Dashed fine girl, Gwendolyn. When do you mean to tie the knot, then? No good waiting too long. Christmas wedding in Town with—"

"My dear, Freddie! I have not yet formally proposed. The engagement is to be announced at Christmas and I should suppose the marriage—"

Peregrine had been listening to this exchange in mounting horror. "But, Good God, sir!" he burst out. "Do you mean we have prevented you from making an offer of marriage?"

"It is of no consequence, Perry," Lord Crichton said calmly. "Miss Phipps-Hedder is a girl of great good sense. She will understand the matter perfectly when it is explained to her." *And it is to be hoped,* he thought to himself, *that her father will be as accommodating.*

"But—" Perry began and was unceremoniously interrupted.

"That's as may be, Beron, but it don't answer the question. Why should Gwen have to understand anything? According to you, you're supposed to be at Radwitch. Why the devil are you going to France, then?"

"My health," said Beron blandly, without opening his eyes.

"Your health! Dash it all, Beron, don't humbug me. There's nothing the matter with your health. You said yourself your leg hardly bothers you. Why, you've the hardest head of anyone I know—never once seen you shoot the cat since I've known you."

Perry had followed this conversation with interest and now he chuckled.

Beron looked at him. "Ah," he murmured, "but that was before I met Peregrine here and his redoubtable sister. Miss Stormont felt a sea voyage would greatly benefit me."

Freddie shook his head as though to clear it. "Can't make sense of it at all," he complained. "What did it signify to you what this Miss Stormont thought?" He nodded towards Perry. "Begging your pardon, an admirable lady as your sister doubtless is, but why should Beron take it into his head to do something just because she suggests..."

"Ah, but Freddie, Miss Stormont is a decisive lady."

"She must be devilish convincing."

"She has her methods."

Freddie still looked unconvinced. "Must be an enormously persuasive woman."

"Miss Stormont scorns halfway measures. She kidnapped me."

"Kidnapped!" Freddie's eyes bulged. He edged away from Perry, rather as if he feared the latter would lay hands on him next. "B-b-b-but," Freddie stuttered, "have you told the captain? Have you got hol-"

"Freddie—" Lord Crichton shook his head "—I should be ashamed of myself for starting such unworthy game."

He waved at Perry. "You tell him, Perry, before an apoplexy takes him off before his time."

LATER, when Beron and Freddie went down to change for dinner, Perry went to find Deborah.

She was pleased and rather apprehensive that Lord Crichton had found himself so recovered. She listened attentively to Perry's account, and having assured herself that the outing had brought no harm, she asked tentatively, "And, er, how did he seem, in himself, I mean?"

"How'd he take being kidnapped, you mean?"

"Perry!"

"You don't need to worry, Debs. He's a great gun, not top-lofty at all. I explained it all to him and he quite saw we had little choice."

"I hope so," Deborah said rather doubtfully.

"Depend upon it. He was scarcely out of curl at all—asked me to call him Beron, in fact." Perry attempted vainly to hide his pride at this mark of noble favour. "And the other passenger, Mr. Wimpole, is an old friend of his, so that's all right and tight, then."

Debs looked at him. Perry's sanguine perceptions were not always to be relied upon. But if Lord Crichton had indeed asked Perry to use his first name, then it did seem unlikely that he was in a passion with them. And yet . . . Lord Crichton was a nobleman of the first stare; he had intended to meet friends in Tillsborough. He could not take kindly to having his plans so cavalierly interrupted—especially by a woman, she thought, remembering his last words to her.

Still, she had done what she thought best. No one could do otherwise. And with this comforting thought, she sent Perry off and went to ready herself for dinner. Not, she thought, that she had much choice in her own preparations. That grey cambric was the best she possessed and it had been perfectly adequate for the few social occasions she had attended in Salisbury. But she had a decided notion it would not do for Mr. Wimpole and Lord Crichton. They must be used to females dressed in the first style of elegance. She had nothing that could possibly...

Come now, Deborah sternly admonished herself, staring into the tiny mirror, *anyone would think you were a Society miss about to make her debut at Almack's.*

This made her chuckle for, of course, she had as much knowledge of Almack's as Perry had of that operadancer's boudoir. It was, therefore, in quite a good temper that she knocked on Perry's door and together they made their way to Captain MacKenzie's dining room.

The gentlemen rose as she entered and Captain MacKenzie conducted her to a place beside him at the round table. On her other side was Mr. Wimpole, then Perry and Lord Crichton on the captain's left. They greeted her politely, but Deborah had the disquieting impression that her arrival had put a damper on the proceedings.

"We're a trifle crowded," the captain said, holding her chair. "But ye'll forgie us, Miss Stormont, for we're nae equipped for four passengers." He nodded to Lord Crichton. "For the leddy, my lord, wouldna leave you to the mercies o'strangers."

"Yes, by Jove!" Freddie looked admiringly at Deborah. "Quite a pickle for you to be in, eh, ma'am?"

"Oh, you wrong Miss Stormont, Freddie. She is a most strong-minded female." Lord Crichton spoke in the lightly ironic tone which Debs found so baffling.

As was her own habit, she masked her uncertainty with stiff propriety. "I am glad to see you well, my lord. I must, of course, ask your pardon if, in the extremity of the moment, my brother and I intervened unwittingly in the conduct of your affairs.''

Beron replied with equal formality. "Not at all, Miss Stormont. I have no doubt as to the dilemma I presented. For the second time, I find myself in your debt." He raised himself in the chair and bowed to her.

For Deborah, dinner was a strained affair. The participants were all too well-bred to permit awkward silences or gaps in the conversation, and Captain MacKenzie kept a paternal eye on her, filling her glass and calling her attention to a choice sweetmeat. But she felt definitely *de trop*. When she rose to leave the gentlemen to their cigars and port, she fancied she heard a collective sigh of relief as the door closed behind her.

CHAPTER FOUR

QUITE A RESPECTABLE PORT, thought Lord Crichton as he watched the captain lift the heavy, broad-bottomed ship's decanter to refill the glasses. In fact, the meal itself had been commendable. It had been simple: just two removes, a pigeon pie and roast capons, with fruit and sweetmeats to follow. But on-board simplicity was to be expected and he'd had much worse meals at inns. He said as much to the captain.

"Thank'ee, my lord. I carry passengers regularly, as Mr. Wimpole here'll tell you, and I strive tae do my best by them. Even," he added, his shrewd eyes twinkling, "a passenger as unexpected as yerself, my lord."

Lord Crichton's answering smile was a trifle wry. "A trip that was as unexpected to me, Captain. I had not thought to be benighted on the open sea, I assure you."

"Ah weel, the best-laid plans gang aft agley."

"But there's always the port." Freddie grinned. "So shove it along here, if you please, Captain."

The captain refilled his own glass, then picked up Perry's. He paused and stared at that young gentleman.

Mr. Stormont lolled back in his chair, one arm flung along the back. He was smiling and nodding to himself. "Good food," he said, "good wine, good frens...all good frens."

Freddie gaped at him. "Devil take it, Beron. We only had four bottles of claret between us and the port is scarcely broached. He can't possibly be *bosky*."

His lordship eyed Perry as the latter continued to mutter, "Good food, good wine, good frens."

"Nevertheless, Freddie, our young friend would appear to have a weak head."

"He's a country lad, forby, and nae accustomed to strong liquor."

"All right, Perry." His lordship pulled Peregrine to his feet. "Time to go."

Perry beamed beatifically at him. "Yes, my lord, Beron, my lord, whatever you say."

"No head at all," said Freddie, shaking his red curls. "Shall I help you, Beron?"

"No, I can manage perfectly. One must only be grateful that he has not become belligerent in his cups."

Indeed, Perry proved perfectly tractable. He allowed Beron to lead him to the cabin, pull off his boots and remove his coat without resistance. He continued to smile happily at the world and to mutter, "Good food, good wine, good frens" with such frequency that his lordship was soon heartily sick of the refrain.

It would be impossible, he considered, to get Perry into the upper bunk, so he manoeuvred his young friend round and heaved him into his own bed.

Perry yawned prodigiously and closed his eyes. His lordship sighed and tiptoed towards the door.

But Perry's eyes flew open again. "Good food," he declared, "good wine, good frens..."

"Good night, Perry," said Beron firmly, and waited. Mr. Stormont fell back on the pillows, his eyes closed again, his mouth opened and a stentorious snore shook the tiny cabin.

Marvelling at the volume of noise the human throat could produce, Lord Crichton closed the door behind him and made for the open air.

At any rate, he'd got the boy safely away before that sister of his saw him castaway. Lord, what a stiff female! And that dress—more suitable for a housekeeper than a gently born lady! Why couldn't she...

But here his lordship's conscience smote him. Evidently the Stormonts were not plump in the pocket. It spoke badly of his own birth and breeding that he should disparage her for such a reason.

There was a slight flush on his cheeks as he stepped out on the passengers' deck. It was, he saw, already occupied. He could not mistake the back of that head, the dark hair pulled so unmercifully into that uncompromising roll. His first impulse was to turn back, but he was still feeling guilty over his uncharitable thoughts. He coughed to alert her and went forward.

Naturally, Deborah had not drunk as much as Perry. But she was utterly unused to alcohol and even a glass and a half of claret had affected her, though not unpleasantly. She was feeling unusually relaxed, and turning to see Lord Crichton, she gave him her most unforced smile yet.

The wind had blown wisps of her hair loose and brought a pink glow to her face. The rather severe lines about her mouth and between her brows were softened by the twilight and her mood.

"My lord," she said warmly. "Pray join me. I have been wondering how you did."

"Thank you, Miss Stormont." He drew up a chair beside hers. "But I believe I am fully recovered—right as a trivet, in fact. You may be easy on my account."

"But I cannot forget that you were on your way to visit friends. Will they not be terribly worried by your failure to appear?"

"They cannot help but be somewhat curious," Lord Crichton replied. So Perry had not told his sister about his, Beron's, aborted proposal. Well, thought his lordship, still in a chastened mood, perhaps it was the best decision. He would not give her further cause for worry. "However," he said aloud, "Captain MacKenzie informs me that he will merely unload his cargo in Cherbourg and return immediately as he can to Dover. I shall go back with him and hope to be with my friends within three days."

"They must, of course, be glad to see you, but surely they will wonder at receiving no word from you?"

"Of course they will," Lord Crichton said easily, "but I trust I shall be able to explain to their satisfaction." He sounded, he reflected, rather more confident than he felt. He certainly did not relish the prospect of the inevitable interview with Sir Rodney.

They sat in a surprisingly comfortable silence, watching the golden track of the sun over the dark green sea. Overhead the pearl grey clouds hung as if painted. The world and time outside the *Orient Wave* seemed to be suspended and there were only the twilight and the silence.

At length, Deborah stirred and sighed. "It is very beautiful out here. I had not imagined it would be like this."

"It is an enchanted time," agreed Beron. "We are not ten hours from England, yet it seems as though we have left that world far behind us."

"Yes, exactly!" Deborah turned eagerly to him. "It is as though one's troubles, one's worries had . . . not precisely evaporated, but somehow shrunk in importance."

"It is always desirable to get a perspective on one's problems," Lord Crichton responded gently. "Sometimes our worries tend to consume us, if we cannot stand back a little.''

At another time and in another place, Deborah might well have remarked tartly on the difference between her very real difficulties and the inevitably trivial annoyances suffered by Lord Auberon Crichton. Now, however, she merely smiled and said, "You are quite right, sir, and what a relief it is to stand back, to be sure!"

"I do not wish to pry into your affairs, Miss Stormont, but whatever your difficulties, if I may serve you in any way, I beg you will not hesitate to call upon me." Lord Crichton was somewhat surprised to hear himself make such a suggestion. He was not entirely clear what had prompted him to do so. However, Deborah's remarks had touched him, and he thought the Society ladies with whom he was wont to associate would never have dreamt of such a conversation. It was refreshing to meet a woman who admitted to thinking of more than clothes, balls and marriage!

Miss Stormont looked away. "I—I thank you, sir, but I must not burden you with my affairs."

"I should not look upon it as a burden." His light, even tone did not vary, but sincerity rang in his voice.

Impulsively Deborah held out her hand to him. "I shall not take such advantage of you, my lord, but I most truly thank you for your concern."

Her hands moved like pale doves in the fading light. He clasped them lightly, then in one swift gesture, he kissed them and released them. "I meant what I said, Miss Stormont."

Deborah flushed. She quickly hid her hands beneath the shawl and pulled it tighter about her. "I—I—" she stammered, scarlet-faced. Determined to change the subject, she glanced about the deck. "I—I wonder where Perry is? I quite expected him to join me."

"Your brother has retired, Miss Stormont."

"Retired? Already?"

"I believe he was feeling indisposed. Some unfortunate persons," Beron continued blandly, "do not easily sustain the motion of a boat."

"Seasick! I had not thought of it. I must—"

"I looked in on him before I came up. He is sleeping. I believe you will do well not to disturb him."

"No, no. You are quite right." She stood up and hesitated for a moment. The relaxed companionship they had shared a few moments earlier had vanished, and now she longed only to get away. "Well, I bid you good-night, my lord." A touch of her formal manner returned. "You have had a bad knock, sir. You, too, will need your rest."

"Yes, madame nurse." He rose and bowed to her, noticing with amusement that she did not offer him her hand again. Indeed, she kept them firmly hidden within that deplorable shawl.

"Good night, sir." Miss Stormont nodded again and quickly vanished.

Beron watched till she had descended the gangway. Then he turned back, stretched out on the chair, folded his hands behind his head and waited for the moonrise. Lord Crichton, it appeared, found very little to quarrel with in his present situation.

Next morning, Lord Crichton and Freddie Wimpole met again at the captain's table.

"How's our young friend?" Freddie grinned as he cut himself a large slice of ham.

"Suffering no ill effects, I believe." Beron helped himself to a more moderate serving of grilled kidneys. "He certainly snored most vigorously last night, and my dressing this morning did not in any way discommode him.''

"He'll have the devil of a head," Freddie predicted.

"Do you know, Freddie, I doubt that. He is very young and bouncingly healthy. I suspect he will shortly be disputing the ownership of that ham with you."

"Then I'd best get my claim in first." Freddie picked up the knife again. "But, I say, Beron, what will you do? We should be in Cherbourg by lunch-time. Will you try to find another passage immediately?"

"The good captain assures me it is his intention to unload and catch the afternoon tide back to Dover, so I shall travel back with him. He has, so he tells me, no other passengers for his return voyage."

"Um." Freddie chomped ham. He cast several glances at Beron. Between bites, he cleared his throat, opened his mouth and, after another pause, shut it again.

Beron watched these proceedings somewhat sardonically. "Spit it out, man, spit it out," he said eventually.

"Spit it out?" Freddie spluttered indignantly. "Why should I spit it out? It's damned good ham."

Beron sighed. "Not the food in your mouth, Freddie, the thought in your head. That is, if you haven't lost it in all the empty space up there."

Freddie laughed. "You're a knowing one, Beron. But I was just thinking..."

"Yes, Freddie," Crichton said patiently. "So I had gathered. But what, pray, is the result of these unusual cogitations?"

"What?" Mr. Wimpole blinked. "Oh! Well, it's this: it's been some time since you've been in France, eh?"

His lordship's fine brows rose. "Very few Englishmen have been in France in these past several years, as you well know. You are among the first to resume regular visits."

"Er, yes." Freddie stared at his depleted plate. He took a deep breath. "Why not come with me, old chap? Aunt's got lots of room in her draughty old place—dashed fine wine available, you know. In fact, just last week in Waitier's, Harewood gave me some Muscadet, the best I've ever tasted. He came across it somewhere in Brittany, he said. I've been thinkin' of trackin' it down, a couple of cases—"

"I'm sure it is a splendid wine, Freddie, but I believe I told you I was promised to the Phipps-Hedders. How discourteous it must be in me simply to fail to appear, especially since they were expecting me for the reason I have already confided to you."

"Well, yes, there's that, too." Freddie nodded vigorously. "That's another reason, ain't it?"

"I fear I am very dull this morning. You'll have to explain, Freddie."

"Come, Beron, you know what Gwendolyn's like. Dashed fine girl," he added hastily. "Nothing against her at all, though I shouldn't have thought she was just in your style. Still," said Freddie fairly, "it's your affair and I'll not meddle."

"Magnanimous of you, Freddie, but can you be a trifle clearer about your point?"

Mr. Wimpole looked puzzled. "Clear? It's perfectly clear, ain't it? I don't know whether you told Gwen what you were up to, but if you didn't, I'll wager old Huff-and-Gruff did."

"That is probably true, Freddie, but—"

"Devil take it, Beron! You're the one who's going to marry her. Don't you know what kind of girl she is?"

"Miss Phipps-Hedder is an extremely well-bred young lady," Beron said stiffly.

Freddie looked at him in exasperation. "Of course she is. What has that to say to anything?"

Beron shook his head. "Freddie, we are at cross purposes here. You are trying to tell me something, though I fear I am too dense to grasp what it is."

"Gwendolyn, man, Gwendolyn! How do you think she's going to feel . . . jilted like this?"

"I have not jilted Miss Phipps-Hedder."

"It'll look like it to her."

"Perhaps, but I have no doubt that she will understand, once she hears my explanation."

Freddie grasped his red curls. "No doubt! Let me tell you then, I have every doubt!"

Beron smiled. "I didn't know you and Miss Phipps-Hedder were such great friends."

"If you ask me," Freddie said frankly, "you don't know much about Gwen—don't eat me, old chap. But even you must realize girl's all excited . . . chap coming up to propose . . . must be a big event in a female's life, after all. And what happens?" Freddie made a dramatic gesture. "Nothing! Chap doesn't show—no letter—nothing! Well, I mean to say, girl's bound to be disappointed, especially a sensitive female like Gwendolyn."

"Of course she is, Freddie. That is what I am trying to tell you, and that is why I must get back to England as quickly as possible."

"Won't do any good." Freddie shook his head. "Remembered when I woke up this morning. Jer—" Freddie stopped and blushed scarlet.

"Well, Freddie," Beron said impatiently, "go on! What did you remember?"

"Jeremy Phipps-Hedder," Freddie gulped. "He's by way of being a chum of mine, you know—anyway, he told me that Gwendolyn's going to France."

"Devil fly away with it!" The uncharacteristic oath escaped Lord Crichton. "You're absolutely right, Freddie. Sir Rodney did tell me that she was to visit friends in France. I had quite forgotten." He made a rapid calculation. "In fact, she is to leave just the very day I should arrive back in Dover."

"Can't propose to a girl on the quays. Ain't the thing at all."

Lord Crichton did not answer. He frowned and tapped his fingers as he considered the situation.

Freddie watched him for a few minutes. "Don't you see, Beron? It's an excellent reason for joining me. Girl's upset, bound to be if she's expectin' you to come up to scratch and you don't appear at all. Go see her in France—bound to impress her—ardent suitor follows her all across the Channel." Freddie paused to admire the picture he had conjured up. "Romantical," he pronounced in considerable satisfaction.

"I cannot conceive that Miss Phipps-Hedder could care for such lending-library nonsense," said Beron coldly.

"Don't you believe it, old chap, Je-Jeremy I mean, says she positively devours novels, whole carriage-loads of 'em trucked in every week."

Still frowning, Lord Crichton studied his friend. He himself had never considered Miss Phipps-Hedder's tastes in reading, or in much else for that matter. Nonetheless, he found himself more than a little out of frame that Freddie—*Freddie,* of all people—should have such knowledge.

"But I can scarcely ride about the countryside demanding news of a visiting English girl. I am sure Sir Rodney mentioned the name of the family she is to visit, but as it was not of the least consequence at the time, I have quite forgotten it."

"Wait a minute." Freddie contorted his face and held up a hand. "Je-Jer told me. Let me think...de...de Keroule...no, no...Got it! De Kéroualle!"

"I believe you are correct, Freddie, de Kéroualle it is. But my objection still holds. France is a big country. It could take me months to locate them."

"Less than forty-eight hours, old chap."

"Do you know them, Freddie?"

"No, but I'll wager Aunt Sophonisba does."

Beron blinked at the name. "Your aunt is acquainted with these de Kéroualles?"

"If she ain't, she'll know someone who is." He saw Beron's enquiring glance. "It's her consuming interest. She'll jaw you dead on the subject of who married who and who's cousin to whom and what family's related to what family and what their grandfather said in 1792." Freddie looked glum. "Shouldn't wonder if that isn't why she sends for me so often: got to keep herself up-to-date on the latest scandal-broth from London. Depend upon it, Beron, my aunt will tell you more about these de Kéroualles that you'll ever wish to know."

Lord Crichton looked unusually indecisive. "I wish I knew what were best to do, Freddie. I must make my apologies to Sir Rodney and Lady Phipps-Hedder. But you may be right. It may be best to repair my fences with Gwendolyn first."

Freddie reached for more coffee. "Ain't like you to make such a piece of work of it, Beron. Send a letter back with MacKenzie presenting your apologies to Sir Rodney. Tell him you're eager to make your peace with Gwendolyn first." He grinned. "That'll give old Huff-and-Gruff time to cool down."

Beron's brow cleared. "Excellent, Freddie. I declare the sea air has improved your headpiece enormously. I shall do that and I shall also send for Eccles to join me here in France."

"Eccles! Never say you've no valet with you!"

"I thought the matter had been explained to you, Freddie. Eccles had gone ahead to Radwitch with my traps."

"My dear old boy." Solicitously, Freddie laid an arm along his friend's shoulder. "You must let me share Walton with you. By Jove, I must have a word with young Stormont. Kidnapping may be all very well, but depriving a man of his valet—that's not good ton, not good at all."

Just at that moment, Perry himself entered the stateroom. He greeted the others rather sheepishly and the colour rose in his cheeks.

"Sit down, Peregrine," his lordship said in his most commonplace tones. "I trust you have recovered from your *mal de mer*." He ignored Freddie's gasp. "Mr. Wimpole and I ought to have warned you that claret is not recommended for persons so affected. Is that not so, Freddie?"

"Eh?" Mr. Wimpole stared, then caught on. "Er, not at all," he responded firmly. "Barley water, that's the ticket, I've always heard."

Perry grimaced. "Ugh! The thing is—" he smiled ingenuously "—I've never been on a boat before, so I had not the least notion of how it might affect me. But," he continued, looking over the table, "I feel quite well this morning, so I must have become used to it." His eye fell on the huge silver platter. "That looks like a dashed good ham."

Lord Crichton did not look at Freddie. However, when Perry had served himself, he said, "How much farther do you go from Cherbourg, Peregrine?"

"I know it's at least one day's journey. My aunt's house is near a town called Redon—but Debs knows better than I."

"Redon!" Freddie looked excited. "Why, my aunt's house is just to the west of Redon. What is your aunt's name, Perry?"

"Madame d'Auray. She is the relic of the Chevalier d'Auray. He was killed in the Terror, you know."

"It was a bloodthirsty time," Lord Crichton commented in his quiet way. "We must hope that more stable times have come to France."

"Madame d'Auray!" Freddie repeated. "But Aunt Sophonisba's mentioned her. She's English, ain't she?"

"Yes, my mother's sister. But I don't think I've heard of your—"

"La Comtesse de Meruvée-Coligny. No, my aunt don't go about." Freddie sighed. "She just sits at home, you know, like a spider, and gathers all the threads together."

Perry looked a little puzzled, then said eagerly, "But if we are to be near to one another, then we may visit back and forth. I don't at all speak French, you know, and shall be glad to see a fellow Englishman."

"By George, yes! And shan't we have good times! For you must know, Perry, Beron's decided to come with us!"

"Have you, sir?" Perry glowed at him. "That is capital news."

"Ain't it?" Freddie agreed enthusiastically. "By Jupiter, to think I was all in the mopes over this trip! Dashed if it doesn't look like being first-rate sport, after all."

Lord Crichton regarded him with his lightly ironic air. "Why, Freddie, I had not imagined that you would have time for anything but your aunt."

"Oh, I shan't have to dance attendance upon her. She's always got some old Tabby to cozen up to her. As long as

I take my chocolate with her in the morning and bring her a posset at night so that she may cross-examine me on all the on-dits, then she don't care what I do. By Jove!'' A thought struck him. ''With the three of us, we're absolutely bound to track down that Muscadet!''

CHAPTER FIVE

"WELL, MISS STORMONT? What are your first impressions of France?" Lord Crichton put down his tankard of cider and looked enquiringly at Deborah.

They were sitting at a rough wooden table set beneath a huge old chestnut tree outside the inn where they had paused for lunch. The sunlight dappled patterns of light over her dark hair, and when she turned her head it glinted suddenly in her ebony eyes.

Lord Crichton had winced at the sight of her poke bonnet, but he acknowledged its necessity. It would have been a crime to mar that ivory complexion by exposing it to the sun. And, he thought, it was nearly as criminal to wear that dreadful shade of puce with such colouring. But perhaps the aunt would be able to effect some changes....

Unaware of his lordship's strictures upon her wardrobe, Deborah was still mulling over his question. At the same time, she, too, was noticing how the sun fell through the leaves onto his hair. It reminded her of how he had first appeared framed in the carriage doorway on the Dover Road. Ordinarily, his hair looked quite black, but the sun gave it a burnished cast. With a start, she realized he was waiting for her to speak.

"Well, my lord, I've seen scarce five hours of it, for I don't count the port which was quite as frenzied as the one in England, even more so to me because this time everyone spoke French, or rather shouted it."

"Your command of the language appeared adequate to the occasion."

"Everyone spoke so fast and I did not understand the accent at all. I have never been more grateful for anything, my lord, than for your arranging for the baggage and the coaches."

"The latter was more the doing of the coachman sent by Freddie's aunt."

Deborah giggled. "Freddie has been talking to me of his Aunt Sophonisba. What a Tartar she must be, to be sure! And what an amazing livery her servants wear. I'd wager that her footman would burst if he puffed out his chest of buttons much farther!"

Crichton glanced at her in surprise. So Miss Stormont possessed a sense of humour. He hadn't thought such a model of propriety could giggle. "The *comtesse* appears to be a lady of decided eccentricity. Freddie is persuaded she must be an acquaintance of your aunt."

"I do not believe my aunt has mentioned her in letters. Her nearest neighbours, so I apprehend, are a widowed *vicomtesse* and her children. To my recollection, I have not heard of a *comtesse*."

"Your aunt herself is a widow, I gather?"

"Yes, it is very sad, is it not? For Brittany is so far from Paris, one would have thought it might have escaped the worst excesses of that terrible Revolution."

"So it must have done, I think," Crichton said gently. "But I do not doubt that there were some extremely unpleasant local effects. However, tell me, Miss Stormont, tell me, how came your aunt to marry a Frenchman?"

"My grandfather met Raoul's grandfather on the Grand Tour. They became friends and maintained a correspondence over the years. Then, when Raoul came to England on his own travels, he visited my grandfather, met my aunt and fell in love with her." Deborah sighed. "They were very happy—until the Revolution."

"Your uncle was in attendance at Versailles, I assume?"

Deborah sipped her wine. It was a delicate rosy colour, with a faint flowery scent. "As I understand the matter, the King was determined to gather all the nobility together at his court."

Beron nodded. "Under his eyes, instead of down in the country, conspiring against him."

"Well, my uncle was not conspiring, but he was by no means interested in the life of a courtier. He was a mere *chevalier*, as you know, so he was not in the first rank of nobility. He hoped to escape the summons to Versailles."

"And did he do so?"

"Almost. But at length he received a direct summons, which of course he could not ignore. He felt obliged to present himself to the King. He had been at court for scarce three weeks when the storm broke and the King himself was forced to flee. In the chaos surrounding those events, my uncle tried to make his way home."

"And your aunt? Was she also in Paris?"

"No, for my uncle had hoped to return very quickly and he had been adamant that she should remain in Brittany." Pensively, Deborah held up her glass, so that the sun sparkled in the rosy depths. "He suspected something of what was to come."

"As an intelligent man, he might well have done," Lord Crichton commented dryly.

"Not quite so intelligent." Deborah sighed. "For all his foresight, he made little provision for my aunt, and when he was killed in one of the skirmishes at the Paris gates, my poor aunt was forced to flee with little more than the clothes she stood up in."

"But she did manage to escape?"

"The countryside was in confusion, for the news from Paris was still very uncertain. My aunt's butler remained loyal and helped her to get through to the coast and thence across the Channel to us in England."

"Alas, in those troubled times, it was not an uncommon story. Your aunt was fortunate in that her estate was still intact."

"I suppose so, though I apprehend that it has suffered from such long neglect."

"Yes, that is not surprising. Ah," Beron said with a nod towards the inn door. "Here come Freddie and your brother."

Deborah looked up quickly. She saw the sun glint on the glasses in their hands. "Oh, dear! Surely Perry has not been drinking so early in the day!" Lord Crichton said nothing at all. Deborah looked at him. His face wore an expression of polite disinterest. Nevertheless, she said rather hesitantly, "I expect you think I am fussing unduly, my lord."

"I should not have the impertinence to comment on your behaviour at all, Miss Stormont."

It was the correct response, but perversely, it drove Deborah to further explanation. "It is just that Perry and I have lived such a retired life so that I fear he is not at all capable of dealing with this sudden..." She searched for the right word.

"Descent into depravity?" The touch of irony was back in Beron's voice. "Believe me, Miss Stormont, no very great experience of vice is needed to cope with a glass of cider before lunch."

Deborah flushed scarlet. She had done it again. She seemed destined to appear a country caper-wit before Lord Crichton.

Freddie came up to them. "Look here, Beron, this is a decentish Muscadet mine host keeps in his cellar." He held an open bottle a few inches below Crichton's nose.

Beron sniffed, but slightly shrugged his shoulders. "It is an attractive bouquet, Freddie, but I'm no expert on Muscadet. What do you think of it yourself?"

"Had a glass. Good, as I said, but not the stuff I'm after." Freddie shook his head. "I'll take a few dozen of this, but it ain't the first-rate article." He looked at the table. "What's that you're drinking, Miss Stormont?" He saw the distinctively shaped, waisted bottle. "Ah! A Côtes de Provence. May I?" At her nod, he lifted the open bottle and sniffed delicately. "A touch heavy on the Carignan, that would be my guess. Don't find it a bit bitter, do you?"

"Nooo." Startled, Deborah stared at her glass. "It seemed very agreeable to me."

"That grape does tend to lose its sharpness as it ages. I'm glad you've got a mellow bottle."

Perry was gazing at Freddie with some awe. "By Jupiter, how do you come by all that knowledge?"

Beron laughed. "Take my advice, Peregrine. Believe implicitly everything Freddie says about wine and mistrust everything he utters about tailoring."

"Here, Beron," Freddie spluttered indignantly.

But his lordship had turned to converse with the landlord. Deborah risked a surreptitious glance at Perry's glass. Perhaps cider was not so very bad?

"What do you advise, Freddie?" Beron asked gravely, but his eyes were laughing. "What shall we drink at lunch? That Muscadet or more of Miss Stormont's rosé?"

"What are we eating, then?" Freddie sat up and looked businesslike. Lord Crichton smiled at Deborah. "It will not be elaborate, Miss Stormont, but I trust you will en-

joy it. It is to be chicken, Freddie, cooked in the style of
Normandy with apples and cream."

"Stay with the Côtes de Provence," Freddie decided
promptly. "There's bound to be some Calvados, apple
brandy," he informed Perry, "in the sauce. Muscadet's a
bit delicate for that. Prefer it with fish dishes myself."

"I feel quite certain you are right," said Beron and
spoke again to the landlord.

Deborah opened her mouth and then shut it again. She
had been going to ask for lemonade for herself and Perry,
but she did not want to embarrass him, or to present herself as even more of a provincial in Lord Crichton's view.
She tried to catch Perry's attention but he was holding his
glass up for the host to fill. He watched intently as Freddie twirled the wineglass to release the bouquet and then
tasted the wine, letting it lie in his mouth before swallowing it. Then he tried to imitate Mr. Wimpole's actions.

Seeing he had a potential disciple, Freddie began to ex-
pound further on the qualities of Côtes de Provence wine.

Well, thought Deborah, taking a tiny sip from her own
glass. Perhaps it was better that Perry be initiated by a
connoisseur. That way he might care for quality rather
than quantity. Though she had heard some disturbing
stories about these London smarts....

"You need not worry, Miss Stormont." Lord Crichton's low voice was definitely amused. "Freddie is an
oenophile, not a drunkard."

This time Deborah looked coolly at him. "I should think
that Mr. Wimpole will behave as a gentleman."

"You may depend upon it, Miss Stormont."

"Beron," Freddie interjected, looking up from his discussion with Perry. "We've been talking about the trip. We
should cross into Brittany early tomorrow and then we

should likely arrive at Perry's aunt's late that afternoon and be at my aunt's in time for dinner."

"Will you stay at the *comtesse*'s before going on to your friends, my lord?" Deborah asked politely.

"For a short while, Miss Stormont."

Probably, Deborah thought, he couldn't wait to see the backs of the Stormont family. Well, she too would be glad to part company with Lord Auberon Crichton. He was far too disturbing a presence.

AFTER LUNCH, they set out again. Though she found the green, rolling countryside pleasant, Deborah had begun to tire of travelling and there was no doubt that the French roads more than lived up to their reputation.

The travelling-coach of the Comtesse de Meruvée-Coligny bounced and bobbed like a cork on a windswept sea. Debs glanced wonderingly at Perry and Freddie. After a few desultory attempts at conversation, those two gentlemen had curled up in their respective corners and were now fast asleep. "How they could," Deborah murmured to herself.

She peeped discreetly out of the window. The second coach, laden chiefly with Freddie's boxes and bags, along with the Stormonts' few, smaller portmanteaux, trundled behind. As well as her coach, the *comtesse* had also dispatched a mount so her nephew might ride if he wished. Lord Crichton was now astride this large, if placid beast, chatting to the coachman of the second vehicle.

A tiny chuckle escaped Deborah. Little as she knew of horseflesh, she could imagine his lordship's feelings at riding such a very unprepossessing animal. She would have liked to tease him about it.

But, she reflected as she sat back, Lord Crichton seemed to find a conversation with the coachman more entertaining than any exchange with her. She sighed and tried to settle herself to sleep. But the movement of the coach had begun to be sickening and her head had begun to throb.

By the time they reached the inn where they were to pass the night, she had a fully fledged migraine. She went directly to her room, where she soon fell into a troubled sleep.

NEXT MORNING, however, she felt much recovered and ready for the last stage of the journey. This time, Perry rode while Beron and Freddie accompanied her in the coach.

"We are in Brittany now," Mr. Wimpole said. "Soon see how it differs from Normandy."

"I see sheep in the fields," Deborah said. "Yesterday, I believe I saw only cattle."

"Dashed good mutton hereabouts," said Freddie enthusiastically. "You'll be sure to enjoy it, Miss Stormont. They roast it with some garlic and some other herbs. Then they—"

Lord Crichton cut ruthlessly through these culinary reminiscences. "There is a milestone giving the distance to Redon and some other villages. Where exactly is your aunt located, Miss Stormont?"

"Beganne St. Pierre," she answered immediately.

"And your aunt, Freddie?"

"Penfag-aux-près. Jaw-breaking names these Frenchies give things."

Lord Crichton's expressive mouth twitched. "Now, Freddie, some of those Frenchies might argue that a man who comes from Willcot Parva-super-Mare is not entitled to complain of their names."

A chuckle escaped Deborah and the twitch at the corner of Beron's mouth grew.

"What's the matter with that?" Freddie demanded. "Plain, straightforward English name."

"Latin, I believe," murmured Crichton. Then his eyes met Deborah's and they both broke into laughter.

"Blessed if I see the joke," said Freddie good-naturedly.

Miss Stormont looked quickly out the window. She did not want to catch Beron's eye again. However, he and Freddie had begun to chat about the last race at this year's Derby. Naturally they made well-bred attempts to include her in their conversation, but, smilingly, Deborah declined to be drawn in.

"Pray continue your discussion, sirs," she said. "I should be glad just to observe the countryside."

The view was certainly worth attention, she considered. Marguerites grew thickly in clumps along the side of the road. The white was picked up by the dots of sheep scattered over the bright green fields. Across the darker green of woods, she caught glimpses of church spires. Occasionally, she saw a pair of imposing iron gates or sometimes even the ornately tiled roof of a château.

But it was the villages that captivated her most. The mellow golden stone houses had front doors which opened directly onto the main street. But if they had no gardens, the Breton villagers more than made up for that lack. Every house, no matter how small, boasted flower boxes at every window. At the entrances and across the fronts, every kind of receptacle—old kettles, stone urns, hollowed-out tree trunks—all displayed a veritable froth of white, pink, red or lavender geraniums.

Deborah was enchanted by the sight and her fingers itched for a pencil. She was making a mental note of all the different colours she had seen, when she realized Freddie had spoken to her.

"Interesting milestone for females, eh?" he said jocularly. "Surprised you're not beggin' us to turn off."

Deborah gazed blankly at him.

"Alençon is some miles to the south, Miss Stormont," Beron remarked in his soft voice.

Deborah's expression did not change.

"A famous lace-making centre, as I'm sure you recall," he added, seeing her lack of response.

"Oh!" Colour flooded her face. "Of—of course. I'm afraid I was wool-gathering."

Freddie laughed. "I'll wager you'd rather be lace-gathering! M'sisters are always ragging at me to bring 'em back all sorts of it—collars, shawls, cuffs, tippets—I don't know what."

Deborah looked down at the tiny strip of plain cotton broderie anglaise that trimmed her own cuffs. Unless there had been some on Mama's things, she didn't believe she had ever seen any Alençon lace, and she certainly couldn't afford to buy it. She looked up and saw Lord Crichton watching her. At the look in his eyes, her face flushed again and she straightened her back. How dared he pity her!

"I say!" Perry had ridden up and now leaned down to the window. "Did you see that milestone back there?"

"Yes, it said Alençon," Deborah replied almost snappishly.

Perry blinked. "Alençon? Are we going there? I thought it was that Saint Pierre Place?"

Conscious of Lord Crichton's gaze, Deborah replied calmly, "Quite right. Have you seen its direction, then?"

"Yes, less than ten miles."

Deborah could not restrain a sigh of relief.

"Tired of being shaken up?" Perry asked sympathetically. "Just hang on, old girl. We're nearly there."

"We shall be there by lunch," Freddie said in satisfaction. "I've been meaning to ask you, Miss Stormont. Do you think we would be imposing on your aunt if we stopped for a while? We should give the horses a rest and—" he wriggled his shoulders "—we could rest ourselves, too! These French roads do bounce one up."

It was impossible to say other than that Madame d'Auray would doubtless be delighted. But as she returned to studying the countryside, Debs realized her delight in the vista had been spoiled. She had hoped she would soon be saying goodbye to Lord Crichton. But, she consoled herself, the parting was only postponed. They were merely stopping for a rest. It would only be a few more hours and she would have seen the last of Lord Auberon Crichton.

CHAPTER SIX

WITH MIXED FEELINGS Deborah watched the miles spin by. Her mind was also turning, back to the days when Madame d'Auray had lived with them in England. In those memories, Tante Louise was a merry, bright-eyed lady who always had time for her young niece and nephew. Now Deborah realized that her aunt must have had many private sorrows, but she had hidden them well from the children.

She could recall, Deborah thought, times when Tante Louise had been very quiet and withdrawn. Then, she and Perry had had to apply all their efforts to win back their familiar laughing companion. Even now, many years later, Deborah could remember how she and her mother had cried together when Louise had decided to return to France. And when, a heart-breakingly few years later, Mama herself had died, Deborah had found great comfort in her aunt's long, loving letters.

But since then, there had been years of turmoil in France. There had been worrisome months when there had been no word at all from Madame d'Auray. Indeed, three years earlier, when Papa had died, it had been close to four months before Louise's shocked response had reached them.

How she longed, she had written, to be with her dearest Debs and Perry. But the political situation was so precarious and travel itself so dangerous that she did not dare to leave the estate she was only then succeeding in bringing back to some kind of order. But she had written to Mr. Shaveley, she told them, to determine exactly how they were left.

Deborah looked out at the pretty countryside and sighed. The news could not have cheered Tante Louise. Poor Papa had let things go to such an extent. They had never been exactly wealthy, but it was only after Mama's death that money had become such a problem.

Increasingly, Papa had retreated to his study. His investments had slipped; an unscrupulous man of business had cheated him; he paid less and less attention to his affairs. Indeed, Deborah had sometimes thought his connection with the world had grown more and more tenuous, so that, at the last, he had loosened the last tie and slipped unobtrusively into death.

When at length Mr. Shaveley had taken over, even that astute gentleman had been able to salvage very little. Deborah smiled sadly as she remembered the concerned face he had presented to her.

"I regret I can see no alternative, Miss Stormont. The debts and liens on the estate are onerous, very onerous indeed. Stormont House must be sold." He shook his head. "Matters have been left in a shocking state, Miss Stormont. I cannot conceal from you my disquiet."

But he had, after gargantuan efforts, managed to save something: a pitiful remainder from what should have been a substantial estate.

"Take my advice," he had urged her, "invest this money in a small cottage. I shall be happy to find a suitable establishment. For after all, you must have somewhere to live."

EVEN IF, Deborah reflected wryly, they had very little to live on. No matter how she scrimped and saved, there never seemed to be enough money. They had only survived this summer because Tante Louise had sent them that bank draft. She pushed her foot reassuringly against the portmanteau safely stowed beneath her seat and then tucked an errant strand of hair back behind her ear. It was Madame d'Auray who had paid for their passage to France. But since Mr. Shaveley had found a tenant for the cottage, perhaps she could use that money to pay back Tante Louise....

She frowned and shifted uneasily in her seat. But what were they to do in the future? She was certainly untrained for anything useful—or lucrative. She had thought of becoming a governess, but she greatly doubted her ability to hold such a post.

And what was to become of Perry? He had spoken once or twice of the army. But they could never afford to buy him a commission. And she felt herself quite terrified by the idea that he might enlist, though honesty compelled her to admit that she could not truly imagine Perry as a soldier.

But this was all old ground. She had been over it so many times. Deborah sighed again. With the back of her hand she rubbed her forehead.

"Is it some time since you've seen your aunt, Miss Stormont?"

Deborah glanced at Beron, but his face showed only polite interest.

"Yes," she said slowly, "it is almost twelve years."

Beron nodded. "I remember when I was invalided out. It was only two years since I'd seen my family—my mother, my uncle, several cousins. But when I came through the door and thought about meeting them all gathered together in the library, I must confess I almost turned tail and ran.''

She chuckled. ''I own I recognize the feeling. But do I understand that you were injured while soldiering, sir?''

''A ball in my leg.'' He held up his hand. ''Pray don't be imagining me a hero, Miss Stormont. Some careless fellow was cleaning his rifle when he discharged it.'' Beron shrugged disparagingly. ''I was unlucky enough to be in the ball's path so—*voilà!*''

''But that is dreadful!'' Deborah exclaimed. ''It must have been, well, humiliating for you.''

Lord Crichton's brows rose, and he gave her a sidelong glance. ''Yes,'' he said dryly. ''You have hit it in the ring, Miss Stormont. Humiliating is precisely what it was—especially to a young hothead who was convinced it was his personal duty to save civilization.'' He smiled a little ruefully. ''But it cured me of that vainglorious nonsense and—'' his smile grew ''—I hope my sense of humour has been equal to the occasion.''

''I don't see—'' Deborah began indignantly, then she stopped. A reluctant twinkle crept into her dark eyes. ''I shouldn't call it humorous exactly, though I suppose one could call it ironic. But are there lasting effects? I have not seen you limp—'' She stopped again. She didn't wish to give the impression she had been studying his lordship.

Beron did not appear to have noticed her confusion. ''No, it has left only a slight weakness in the leg. It bothers me only when I become excessively tired. I should think myself a poor sort indeed if I were to complain of such a trifling inconvenience when others suffered much more serious injury.''

''I say! I say! Debs! Freddie! Beron!'' Perry's excited face appeared at the window and Freddie awakened from his nap.

"What's all the row, old chap?" he asked, yawning.

"We're here!" Peregrine announced. "We're in Beganne St. Pierre! There's the marker ahead."

Freddie leaned out of the window. "There's a château over there," he said. "I can see turreted roofs."

"That's not my aunt's house," Deborah said quickly. "We have to go through the village for that. Le Bois qui Chante is a few miles beyond the actual village."

"Le Bois qui Chante?" Lord Crichton repeated. "That is a charming name." He saw Mr. Wimpole wrinkling his brow. "The Singing Wood, Freddie."

"I apprehend that it is so named because of the surrounding poplars," Deborah said.

"Look!" Freddie cried. "Here are the first houses!"

Beganne St. Pierre was a delightful town. The Ille river ran through its centre, presenting them with a picturesque vista of winding banks and arched stone bridges. Some of the houses were clearly very old. Their timbered upper stories leaned out precariously over the street.

"Good thing we haven't a great pile of boxes on the second carriage," Perry said, instinctively ducking his head.

The villagers were about their daily business but many of them stopped to stare at the visitors. Deborah regarded them with equal interest. The women, she saw, wore black dresses, topped with white aprons decorated with elaborate ribbon designs. On their heads, many wore high white caps, like cylinders of white lace.

As they passed the last of the houses, Peregrine spurred his horse ahead. The knots in Deborah's stomach increased. It was absurd, she told herself, to feel so anxious about meeting Tante Louise—dear, kind Louise. But what, she asked herself in sudden desperation, what if Louise couldn't help them?

She felt a light touch on her hands. With a start she looked down. Her fingers had pressed so firmly on the back of her other hand that they had left angry red patches.

It was Lord Crichton who had touched her. For a moment he let his hands cover hers. Then he squeezed them—so lightly and so quickly that she almost believed she had imagined the gesture. But it had helped her overcome her rising panic. She made her hands relax in her lap.

Lord Crichton was brushing a minuscule crease out of his sleeve. He was wearing one of Freddie's coats, and it strained a little across his shoulders. But he wore the borrowed clothes with his usual air of quiet elegance.

Deborah was grateful he had neither spoken nor looked directly at her. But she had felt his support. She drew a deep breath and was about to speak when Perry's voice broke in.

"We're here! We're here!" His excited face appeared at the window. "We just turn to the left here. Do look, Debs."

The coach turned and Deborah saw a wide entranceway, flanked by two rather plain pillars, surmounted by huge stone urns full of mauve geraniums.

They followed a long road lined by tall poplars and came out on a circular driveway in front of a square stone manor-house.

A rod of intricate ironwork ran the length of the grey tiled roof. On either side of the door were five sets of symmetrically arranged windows, each with a pair of white painted shutters. Below each of the ground-floor windows, a stone trough overflowed with the same pale purple flowers.

Heart thumping, Deborah glanced up. She met Lord Crichton's gaze. His grey eyes were warm and encouraging. He sketched a small salute in the air. Deborah laughed, and the coach came to a halt by a mounting block a little distance from the front entrance.

"Do hurry up, Debs! I think I can see Tante Louise waiting for us."

Deborah stepped out onto the first step. She did not notice that her unfashionably full skirt still trailed on the coach floor. Almost fearfully she looked to the front door. A small, white-haired lady was waving enthusiastically and started towards them at a run.

"Tante Louise!" Debs herself waved frantically and made to jump down from the block. Her skirt caught somewhere, and she tugged it impatiently. There was a muffled cry behind her and a heavy body brushed past, knocking her into Perry's arms.

"What is it?" she gasped, holding on to her brother. "What's happening? What's..." her voice trailed off. Both she and Perry stood transfixed as Lord Auberon Crichton toppled off the steps and crashed to the ground before them.

"Oh, no!" Deborah wailed, clutching Perry's arm. "Not again. *Oh, no!*"

"Now, my love, you must not be overcome." Aunt Louise spoke in the placid tones Deborah remembered and she turned gratefully to her aunt. Madame d'Auray beckoned to her butler standing respectfully behind her.

But Lord Crichton had raised himself on one elbow. He shook his head, disarranging his thick black hair. "Whaaat...?" His eye fell on Deborah. "Miss Stormont!" His other hand went to the side of his head. "Not again. Oh, no!"

"Lord Crichton," Deborah began, "I can't tell you how sorry I am. I assure you..."

His lordship held up his hand and she stopped. Still holding up his hand, as though to ward her off, he tried to heave himself up. But his right leg buckled under him.

"Oh, no!" Deborah wailed again. "His bad leg!"

"Here, old chap." Freddie had pushed his way down the block and now grasped his friend's arm. The butler slipped to Beron's other side and discreetly supported him there.

"My lord," said Madame d'Auray, "I am naturally appalled that such an accident should occur just as you arrive at my house. I beg you to rest here awhile. I shall send instantly for the doctor. In the meantime, please permit Bigard, here, to tend you. He has an excellent knowledge of herbal and medicinal matters." She nodded to Bigard, and he and Freddie began to lead Lord Crichton towards the house.

"Does it hurt badly, old chap?" Mr. Wimpole asked solicitously.

"Damnably," said Lord Crichton between clenched teeth.

Freddie cast an anxious look at him. "Perhaps we should get a stretcher...."

"No, Freddie. I didn't need a stretcher in the French wars, and I'm damned if I'll let that female drive me to one."

Fortunately, it was a short distance to the house. Mounting the stairs, however, was a trickier proposition, but at last Lord Crichton sank into a huge armchair in a large bedroom. He lay back and shut his eyes.

"Brandy, please," Freddie hissed at the butler and the man nodded and withdrew.

Freddie knelt by his lordship's chair. "Beron, old chap, I'm going to see if I can pull these boots off."

"Don't *cut* them off." His lordship essayed a grin. "I can wear your coats and shirts, Freddie, but I certainly cannot get into your boots."

To his relief, Freddie was able to get the boots off without resorting to a knife. He hoped he hadn't hurt his friend too much, but there was no doubt his lordship was very pale. His mouth was a thin, taut line.

"Ah!" He looked up thankfully as the butler entered with a decanter and glasses on a silver tray. Behind him, two rather frightened-looking maids carried basins, ewers and cloths.

Freddie grabbed a glass and filled it. "Here you are, old chap. Try this."

His lordship gulped some brandy, and a little colour returned to his face.

The butler put down the tray and spoke rapidly to the maids in a language Freddie did not understand at all. Breton, he supposed. The girls deposited their burdens and scurried off.

Bigard gently lifted Beron's foot onto a footstool and began to prepare a bath with the hot water and some dried herbs.

"Freddie," his lordship said, sitting up straighter. "Does that door lock?"

Freddie stared. "It's got a key, all right, Beron, but you don't need to worry about that, old chap—"

"Then turn the key, Freddie!"

Mr. Wimpole hesitated.

"I am not delirious, Freddie. Oblige me by locking the door, if you please."

Shrugging slightly, Freddie obeyed.

His lordship relaxed a little. The butler had removed his stocking and was now easing his foot into the basin. Bigard scattered more herbs in the water and a sharp, invigorating scent filled the room.

Beron smiled more easily. "Truly, Freddie, I am not wandering in my mind. I am merely bent on self-preservation. I don't want that woman in here."

"What woman, old chap?"

"Miss Deborah Stormont. She's nearly assassinated me twice! I'm damned if I'll provide her with a third opportunity!"

CHAPTER SEVEN

UNSEEINGLY, Deborah looked around. Her aunt's pretty sitting room was a blend of English and Breton taste. The comfortable, chintz-covered sofas and chairs were in a familiar style. Against one wall was a huge armoire of dark wood, decorated with silver nail-heads and incised designs. A stone arch, complemented by a snowy frill of lace, led into a cosy little library.

But though she stared at all these things, Deborah's mind took in none of them. Her thoughts were still on that shattering scene by the mounting block.

Madame d'Auray was pouring tea into a set of vividly painted cups. Fleetingly, Deborah noted plates in the same pattern glowing against the dark wood dresser.

"Here you are, my dear." Her aunt handed her a cup. "Drink it," she urged kindly, "and try to compose yourself. It was, after all, an accident."

"But the second one!" Deborah cried, anguished. Somewhat disjointedly, she began to tell her aunt the story of their acquaintance with Lord Crichton.

As Madame d'Auray listened, her dark eyes grew steadily brighter, and there was the tiniest quiver at the corner of her mouth. However, when she spoke, her voice was admirably grave. "Nevertheless, I cannot think you culpable, Debs. His lordship was no doubt put out by the change in his plans, but from what you say, he has never blamed you." She picked up a small basket from beside her chair and extracted a length of intricate crochet.

"No," Deborah admitted, sipping her tea.

"Even though—" the twinkle became more pronounced "—your actions were perhaps a trifle high-handed?"

"Tante!" Deborah put down her cup. Then she caught her aunt's eye. "Oh, well," she admitted reluctantly, "I suppose you're right. But," she added, her voice trembling a little, "but, oh, Tante Louise, I didn't know what to do!"

Madame d'Auray did not say anything, but she put down her cup and immediately embraced her niece.

As the familiar scent of lilies of the valley surrounded her, Deborah gave a watery sniff. Then her defences crumbled and she burst into tears.

Madame let her cry for a few minutes as she patted her shoulder. Then she reached for a handkerchief.

"Thank you, Tante Louise." Deborah wiped her cheeks. "I'm so sorry. I don't know what came over me."

Her aunt gave her another hug and then poured more tea. There was a faint frown between her brows. The last years had clearly been even more difficult for Deborah than she had imagined.

"Tante Louise!" Perry pushed open the door and entered in his usual exuberant way. "The doctor chap's just arrived. Your butler's taken him up."

Madame smiled fondly at him. "Thank you. Will you have tea, Perry?"

Peregrine threw himself into an armchair. "Lord no, thank you. I'll not maudle my insides with that stuff." He looked thoughtful. "Don't know what it'd do to my palate, either."

"Do you have a palate, Perry?" his aunt asked with interest. "I congratulate you."

Perry tried, but failed to look modest. "Freddie says I have a natural talent."

"Mr. Wimpole is obviously a young gentleman of perception."

"Yes, but it's rather too bad he has to go off to that aunt of his. I hope we shall be able to see a lot of him despite her."

"Mr. Wimpole has an aunt in France?"

"Yes, Tante," Deborah put in, "and Freddie thinks that you may know her. She is the Comtesse de Meruvée-Coligny."

"Sophonisba? Good gracious me!" Madame's eyes opened wider. "Then your Mr. Wimpole must be her English nephew. I have heard her speak of him often."

Remembering Freddie's remarks on his aunt, Deborah said, "I collect that the *comtesse* is, er, rather an Original?"

Tante Louise chuckled. "One might say so. She is certainly a formidable old lady. She never leaves her house, but she knows everything about everyone for miles around. And about their grandparents and great grandparents, too, I expect."

"She's bound to know these de Keroualles, then?" Perry had found a rather curious, soldier-shaped nutcracker. He was attempting to fit a nut into the top of the soldier's head.

"De Keroualles?" Debs repeated. "Who may they be, Perry? I didn't think you knew anyone in France?"

"Oh, I don't know 'em." Carefully, Perry slid the hat down and smiled in satisfaction as the nutshell shattered. "But it seems Beron's fiancée is visiting them."

Deborah's hand moved convulsively and her teacup clattered against the saucer.

For a moment, Madame d'Auray eyed her niece; then she turned to Perry. "Lord Crichton is affianced, then?"

Perry swallowed the last piece of hazelnut and picked up another. "It ain't official yet. In fact—" he grinned at Deborah "—he was on his way to pop the question formally when Debs here press-ganged him."

"Perry!" Deborah was very pale. "Do you mean we've prevented Lord Crichton from making a proposal of marriage?"

"You don't need to fly into the boughs over it, Debs. He don't mind." Perry snapped down the hat again. "Come to think of it, it's actually all worked out for the best, after all."

His sister did not look as if she shared this sentiment. She pressed one hand to her temple. "What he must think of us—of me! I had no idea—"

Madame d'Auray held up a hand. "Now, *ma chère,* do not upset yourself again. Naturally you could not know Lord Crichton's intentions. But do I collect from what Perry says that this young lady is staying with the de Keroualles?"

"Yes." Perry was picking out the shell pieces from another nut-meat. "So Beron's come to see her here, and as I said, it all works out much better that way. Now he may join up with Freddie and me—much better than hanging on some female's skirts." He held out his hand. "Care for a hazelnut, Debs?"

Deborah looked despairingly at her aunt. "I don't know how he can bear to be civil to me. Not only have I spoilt his marriage plans, but now I have delayed him further and no doubt taken him even more out of his way."

"If he and the young lady are truly in love," said Madame d'Auray placidly, "then a slight delay will not unduly discommode them. Nor have you taken him out of his way; quite the opposite, in truth."

Both the Stormonts stared at her.

"The Vicomte de Keroualle, his mother the *vicomtesse* and his sister are my nearest neighbors."

"If that don't beat all!" Perry beamed at her. "We shall all be neighbours, then—Freddie, Beron and us. What splendid times we shall have, to be sure."

For some time now, Deborah had been conscious of continuing background noises. She looked vaguely about the room, then her gaze fixed on the long French doors. She gave a little shriek. "Look!"

Her aunt followed her pointing finger and clucked in annoyance. "Oh, dear, we have been so distracted that I quite forgot the Duchesse." She got up and opened one of the windows.

The Stormonts watched, fascinated, as a large white goat, with unusually long, silky hair, stepped daintily into the room. It surveyed them coldly from strange, liquid-gold eyes.

Madame d'Auray poured some tea into a saucer, added some milk and then a lot of sugar. She placed the saucer on the floor. The goat snorted and began to lap up the tea with a bright pink tongue.

Madame d'Auray looked a trifle guiltily at her niece and nephew. "She was orphaned as a kid and I fed her with bottles. We call her Duchesse, after the famous and much beloved Duchesse Anne of Brittany, you know." She shrugged comically. "I'm afraid she doesn't realize she's a goat. She's a Kashmir, pure-bred, with an enormous pedigree. I think she feels the rest of us are rather under-bred."

The goat looked up, switching her regal head from side to side. She bestowed one last, haughty blink on the Stormonts, sniffed disparagingly and trotted out.

Perry and Deborah laughed, as much at their aunt's air of embarrassed pride as at the top-lofty goat.

The butler came noiselessly into the room.

"Ah, Bigard, is *monsieur le médecin* finished?" Louise asked in French.

The butler spoke to her in the same language. He spoke rapidly and in an accent unfamiliar to Deborah. She caught mention of *le médecin* but she thought there was something else troubling the butler. She heard him repeat the word *rôdeur,* but she did not recognize the word and could not follow enough of the conversation to guess at the meaning. Tante Louise, she thought, seemed irritated rather than upset by his report.

"Is something the matter, Tante?" she asked as the butler bowed and took his leave.

"Not really, my dear. It is an occasional, if rather trifling occurrence at the Bois and at the château—treasure-hunters!"

"Treasure-hunters!" Perry sat up. "Whatever do you mean?"

But at that moment, the door opened again and Bigard ushered in a tall, thin man with a grave manner. "*Monsieur le médecin,*" he murmured before he shut the door.

Madame greeted the doctor and introduced her niece and nephew. Perry's French did not extend much beyond *bonjour,* but Deborah found it easy to follow the doctor's slow, precise speech.

Non, the English milord was not seriously injured, but it was necessary that he should repose himself for some days. He must remain tranquil. The leg was not broken but it was much swollen. There was, he understood, already a weakness there. *La guerre,* one supposed.

In any case, milord was in much pain now, but he had provided something for that. If he found himself better in the morning, milord might get up and promenade himself a little, but with the aid of a stick, *naturellement.* But he was to be careful and to rest himself often.

In two days' time the doctor would have the honour of attending upon milord again. Punctiliously, he shook hands with everyone again and bowed himself out, just as Freddie reappeared.

Mr. Wimpole bowed to his hostess. "Dashed bad form, ma'am," he said, "introducin' myself after marchin' into your house without so much as a by-your-leave."

"You had, of course, to concern yourself with your friend." Madame gestured him to a seat.

"Kind of you to say so." Freddie accepted a cup of tea. "That doctor johnny certainly knows his job. Beron's sleeping like a baby now."

Deborah leaned forward. "Mr. Wimpole, I can't tell you how I regret my clumsiness. I hope Lord Crichton is not furiously angry with me."

Freddie gulped tea. He looked sideways at Debs and remembered Beron's comments on that lady. "Ah! Well, I, er, of course he ain't, Miss Stormont. Beron ain't the sort of chap to get in a passion over an accident—nobody's fault after all." Devoutly, Freddie hoped Miss Stormont would not take it into her head to visit his lordship in the near future. He did not know which would be worse for her to encounter: the locked door, or Beron in his present mood. "He's sleeping now," he repeated. "Doctor chappie says he's not to be disturbed."

Deborah was about to speak, but Perry forestalled her. "Of course Beron ain't in a pet, Debs! He knows it wasn't your fault."

Miss Stormont looked dubious. She rather feared Perry was being too sanguine.

Perry was struck by a sudden memory. "I say, Tante Louise, I remember your telling us stories about the huge cellars here in the Bois. Did any of the old bottles survive the troubles?"

"Thanks to Bigard, there was very little looting of the house," Madame d'Auray said. She smiled at Freddie. "You have been tutoring my nephew in wine appreciation, I collect."

Freddie blushed a little. "My pleasure, ma'am. Perry's got an instinct for it, I must say."

"Then perhaps you two would like to explore the cellars? You could choose a wine for dinner, if you wish. Bigard already has some cooling for lunch, but do consult with him about tonight."

"Never meant to plant ourselves on you like this, ma'am." Freddie's sensibilities were clearly lacerated by these unconventional proceedings. "But we can't jaunter off until Beron is feeling more the thing. Shall have to continue to trespass on your hospitality, ma'am."

"You do not trespass at all, Mr. Wimpole. Naturally you will stay until his lordship is ready to travel. If you desire it, I shall have a message sent to your aunt."

Freddie's face had begun to brighten, but now he frowned again. "Aunt Sophonisba? Yes, yes, I had best do that. But does this mean that you are acquainted with my aunt, ma'am?"

"I am not an intimate of hers. But we have met and I take tea with her on occasion."

"And Tante Louise knows these de Keroualles too, Freddie," Perry put in. "You'll never guess—they're her neighbours! So Beron won't have to worry about finding them. What a piece of luck, eh?"

"Yes, Mr. Wimpole," said Deborah eagerly. "And perhaps we should also send a message to his lordship's fiancée. She will be worried if she hears of his accident. Indeed perhaps she may wish to come here and assure herself—"

"Steady on, Miss Stormont." Freddie blinked at her. "Don't even think Gwendolyn's arrived in France yet. As for sending messages—well, take my advice, don't do anything till we ask Beron just what he'd like."

"Naturally we shall not," said Madame d'Auray as she rose to her feet. "Now I am going to take Deborah up to her room. I've had lunch put back so you two will have time to investigate the cellars before you change." She nodded at the two gentlemen and shepherded Debs out of the room.

"I'm afraid I haven't much to change into," Deborah said as she followed her aunt upstairs.

"I understand," the older woman said kindly. "But I notice that Peregrine is quite acceptably turned out."

Deborah flushed. "At that age clothes matter so much," she muttered.

Madame d'Auray found the door she was seeking and stopped with her hand on the white porcelain doorknob. She looked back at her niece, her gaze resting thoughtfully on the puce gown that had so dismayed Lord Crichton. Her voice was very gentle when she said, "You have had a lot to bear with in the past few years, my dear. But now that you are finally here, I hope you will let me share some of those burdens." She opened the door and gestured Debs inside.

Miss Stormont stopped dead, her eyes on the vast bed, which took up the whole of one long wall. "W-whatever is that?" she asked, her voice faltering.

Her aunt chuckled. "It is rather overwhelming, isn't it? It's a Breton *lit enclos*. Those drawers underneath are for storage, of course. And while you won't need them now, the bed curtains will keep out the winter draughts."

"It looks as though I shall need a ladder to climb into it."

"Not a ladder exactly, but there is a set of steps. Now, you've had a trying morning, my love. Lie down for a while and I shall send a maid up later with some tea. She will help you to dress for lunch."

"Oh, no, Tante Louise! Not a maid! I mustn't upset your household."

"*Doucement, doucement, ma chère.* There is no need for such flights. You are not in any way upsetting my household. But if you refuse Marie-Claire's services, then I can't answer for the consequences."

"Marie-Claire?"

"She is Bigard's daughter. She is an ambitious girl. She wishes to look after a *grande dame* in Paris, but naturally, her parents will have none of this. Marie-Claire, however, regards your coming as a stepping-stone to the great career that inevitably awaits her."

Deborah laughed. "I see it would be most unkind in me to deprive her of her chance. So I thank you, Tante Louise—" her voice quavered "—for that, and for everything."

"Now, now." Madame gave her a quick hug. She helped Deborah to slip out of her dress. "There, *ma petite*," she said, as she went up the set of heavy wooden stairs after her niece. She tucked the lavender-scented sheets about her.

"Rest for a while." She touched Debs lightly on the forehead. "And no more worrying."

Deborah smiled as her aunt left. That was sometimes easier to say than to do. She couldn't, it sometimes seemed to her, remember a time when she hadn't had to worry. There was the matter of Lord Crichton, for instance.

He might be soft-voiced and elegantly mannered, but Deborah had a strong suspicion a great deal more than was outwardly visible went on beneath that polished exterior. Still, his fiancée was nearby. That should be some consolation.

Oddly, as she contemplated this thought, Miss Stormont herself derived little comfort from it. However, Madame d'Auray was right. It had been a demanding morning and the days of travel had taken their toll. Deborah sighed, turned and was asleep.

CHAPTER EIGHT

WHEN LORD CRICHTON AWOKE the next morning, his head was quite clear. Experimentally, he moved his leg. There was a dull ache there, but he found that encouraging after the throbbing agony of yesterday.

He sat up and surveyed the bedroom. It was the same one he recalled rather indefinitely from last night. He should be grateful, he reflected sardonically, that Miss Stormont had not spirited him off to yet another country overnight.

Someone coughed discreetly at the door. It was Walton, Freddie's valet. He carried a number of garments carefully folded over his arm. "Good morning, my lord," he said. "May I enquire as to how you find yourself this morning?"

"Surprisingly well, Walton. But what is all this? Is Mr. Wimpole culling his wardrobe?"

"In a manner of speaking, my lord. Since we are leaving this morning, Mr. Wimpole begs that you will accept these few shirts and coats to tide you over till your lordship's own supply may be replenished."

"I'm afraid," said Beron ruefully, "that it will be another two or three days at the earliest before I can hope to see Eccles with my own clothes. I am very much in Mr. Wimpole's debt. Please convey my gratitude to him."

"I shall, my lord. However, Mr. Wimpole will do himself the honour of visiting your lordship later this morning." He paused as a maid in a black dress, white apron and intricate lace cap entered. She bobbed a curtsy as she set down a tray.

When she had left, Walton continued in his stately way. "I shall leave your lordship to the enjoyment of your lordship's breakfast. When Mr. Wimpole has finished dressing, I shall return to assist your lordship." He bowed and retired.

Reflecting that, together, Walton and Miss Stormont possessed enough starch to last French laundresses for six months, Beron picked up the bowl of creamy coffee. He hobbled over to the window and sat down to enjoy the view and his breakfast.

True to his word, Walton returned and was just easing Beron into a borrowed cot when Freddie came in.

"Can you bear to watch, Freddie?" Beron cocked a quizzical eyebrow at his friend. "Once it's been forced across my shoulders, this coat will never be the same again."

"Think nothing of it, dear old chap. Glad to be of service. What's a few shirts?"

"And coats and cravats and a pair of buckskin breeches."

Freddie dismissed these garments with a wave of his hand. "Sure you don't want any more? Brought a number with me, don't you know."

"You must have brought a whole tailor's shop," Beron said frankly. "But I am truly grateful to you. Miss Stormont did not consider my wardrobe when she decided I should enjoy a sea voyage."

"Um! Yes, well." Freddie fiddled with a brightly painted china candlestick. "She was quite cut up about what happened yesterday, you know. Sends her deepest regrets and all that."

"She can't regret the whole thing half as much as I do," replied Beron grimly.

"Got some good news, though." Freddie attempted to give his friend's thoughts a happier turn. "Our hostess knows these de Keroualles—they're her neighbours. No need for you to rush about France, after all."

"There would be no need for me to *be* in France at all if it were not for that extraordinarily interfering female!"

Mr. Wimpole looked closely at his lordship. It wasn't like Beron to be so mumpish. "Leg botherin' you this morning?" he asked solicitously.

"Not at—" Beron stopped, a rather guilty look on his face. "No, Freddie, I have no such excuse for my crotchets. Pray forgive me."

"Don't mention it, dear old fellow. But I'm glad to hear the leg is mending. I've got to be off to my aunt's, you know. The old girl will be all of a twitter, wonderin' what's become of me."

From what he'd heard of the countess, Beron thought this an unlikely description. However, he did agree that Freddie must hasten to pay his respects to his relative.

"But I shall be back," Freddie assured him. "Madame d'Auray has kindly invited me to visit as often as I wish."

"Then, for heaven's sake, Freddie, take advantage of the invitation!" Beron heaved himself to his feet to shake hands. "Don't leave me to the mercies of the Stormont female."

As he went downstairs, Freddie shook his head. Beron certainly seemed to have taken Miss Stormont in dislike. No accounting for it, really, Freddie thought. Miss Stormont might be a bit stiff sometimes, but she was a good sort and she and Beron had seemed to get along all right earlier—even laughed at the same incomprehensible jokes. He shook his head again.

Freddie had not been the only early-morning visitor at the Bois that day. Just as he was saying farewell to Beron, Madame d'Auray was greeting her niece.

"I hope you slept well, *ma chère,*" she said, sitting in a heavily carved chair by the great bed.

"Very well, Tante, thank you. And—" Deborah indicated the tray across her knees "—such luxury will quite spoil me."

"That is my intention." Aunt Louise smiled fondly at her. "What pretty hair you have, dearest. Why do you wear it in such a severe style?"

Deborah pushed a thick lock behind her ear. "Well, it saves trouble, you know," she explained rather apologetically.

"Marie-Claire has a way with hair. I wish you would let her try arranging it."

"Certainly, if you wish it, Tante."

Louise's eyes twinkled. "Now don't tell me you don't care at all how you look!"

Deborah laughed. "Of course I do! I'm not such an unnatural female. But—" she paused and the lines between her brows reappeared "—there hasn't been—well, to put the matter plainly before you, Tante, there hasn't been the money for me to indulge in fashion and such fribbles."

Madame d'Auray squeezed her niece's hand. "Let me explain the situation here to you, Debs. The last few years have been more difficult than I ever imagined. It has taken me a long time and there have been many setbacks to get the estate into some kind of working order again." She sighed a little. "I am, of course, grateful that there was very little damage to the house and land, but my major difficulty has been a lack of funds."

Deborah looked swiftly at her aunt.

"Now don't let your imagination run away with you, child. We are not in any way rolled up. It's just that until the estate is truly back on its feet, our funds are rather limited."

"Then . . ." Deborah hesitated and put down her bowl of coffee. "Then it is quite unconscionable for Perry and me to—"

"Deborah!" Madame d'Auray's tone was unusually peremptory. "That is precisely what I am *not* telling you. I am merely explaining that while I should love to take you to the most stylish coiffeur and to the most elegant modiste, I simply cannot do so at present. But—" she drew herself up and almost glared "—I am certainly more than able to provide a home for you and Perry and I certainly intend to do so, so pray do not argue."

Deborah giggled. Her aunt reminded her of an enraged rabbit, with her bright eyes and white curls. "All right, Tante Louise, I shan't say another word, just how very gra—"

"Pooh!" Louise began to calm down a little. "Let us talk of something else then."

"There was something I meant to ask you about last night. Bigard was telling you something about a '*rôdeur*,' at least I think that was the word. What does it mean, Tante?"

Madame d'Auray made her little click of annoyance. "It means prowler. Oh, don't be alarmed. It's just another of those treasure-hunters I mentioned."

"But—" Deborah wrinkled her brow "—is there a treasure at the Bois?"

"At the Bois, or up at the château. At least that's the story." She got up and wandered over to the window. "In an odd sort of way, it's connected with what we were just discussing. Raoul, my husband, you know, was convinced that a cataclysm was inevitable. He was great friends with the *vicomte,* Edouard's father, I mean. Together they tried to plan for the upheaval they knew was coming."

"How could they do that, Tante?"

"Raoul told me he was gathering all the money he could and turning it into silver, gold and jewels." She sighed. "He felt sure we should have to flee and such precious, portable things would be best to take with us."

In deference to her aunt's memories, Deborah was silent for a few moments, then she said rather hesitantly, "But... his plans did not work out?"

Madame d'Auray sighed again. "He was called to Versailles. He thought there was still time. He thought he would come back and..."

Deborah threw back the clothes and ran to her aunt. "I'm so sorry, dearest Tante," she said, hugging her. "I did not mean to bring back unhappy memories."

"No, no." Louise blew her nose. "I want to tell you." She let Deborah lead her back to a small sofa. "That's what he thought, but as you know he never did return to the Bois."

The two women sat in silence for a long moment. Then Louise shook her white curls. *"Eh bien,"* she said, *"Revenons à nos moutons!* Where was I?"

Deborah was still thinking. "The gold and other things," she said, "what happened to those, Tante?"

Madame d'Auray shrugged her slight shoulders. "I do not know."

Deborah stared at her.

Louise smiled. "In many ways my poor Raoul was still a boy. He enjoyed his secrets very much and I...I was not sure that he was right in his fears. You must remember that life in Beganne St. Pierre was going on much as usual. We

heard rumours from Paris, but that was so far away...."
She smiled sadly. "It seemed impossible that anything
should touch us here. Raoul and the *vicomte* had always
loved games, puzzles, ciphers. They made up riddles to
tease each other and they invented a code in which they
wrote to each other. I'm afraid I thought Raoul's fears
about the future were really just a part of one of those
games."

"But it was true, tragically true."

"Yes, my dear, it was true and the truth caught up with
us before we were ready."

Deborah hugged her aunt again. "Don't talk about it
any more, dearest. Not if it makes you sad."

"I shall tell you the end of the story, as far as I know it,
at least. Now, you asked about the treasure—"

"Yes, and if you haven't got it, what happened to it?"

"Any number of things, I should imagine. Perhaps it
was hidden somewhere. That's what the fortune-hunters
think, no doubt—it's a story that won't go away. But I
myself think that Raoul brought it with him. He could
easily carry such things in a strong-box. Perhaps it was
stolen after he was killed—divided up amongst the mob."

"And the *vicomte*? Didn't you say he and my uncle
worked together? Did he not know what had happened?"

"If he did, he did not say so, neither to me nor to the
vicomtesse. He travelled to Paris with Raoul. He was im-
prisoned in the Bastille and later executed. If he brought
his valuables with him, I have little doubt his treasure was
scattered amongst a Paris mob or used up in a vain attempt to buy his freedom." Louise stared into the past
again, then she straightened her back. "The story of the
missing or hidden treasure has become very well-known in
the neighbourhood. I suppose it lends a rather romantic air
to us all."

"But no one has ever found a trace of the lost treasure?"

"Not a trace of it. Bigard was able to save this house from too much damage, but I have never found any treasure here. As for the château, it was thoroughly ransacked and nothing was found there either."

"But people still come searching for it?"

"I expect that our recent *rôdeur* is due to the *vicomtesse*'s recent discovery."

Deborah looked excited. "You mean she found a clue?"

"A clue?" Madame d'Auray's tone was dry. "I suppose it might be so described, but to what I couldn't say."

"Do tell me what it was, Tante."

"The *vicomtesse* has an old desk—a pretty piece, but needing some restoration. In the course of the work, a secret compartment was found."

Deborah's eyes were bright with anticipation. "Tante, this is just like a romance! What did the *vicomtesse* find?"

"I'm sorry to disappoint you, my dear. Most of what she found were rather prosaic bills and letters."

"Most? But not all?"

"There was a copy of a rhyme, which was not new to me, because I had also seen a copy of it in Raoul's papers. But the workmen who found it spread the story and it has certainly fuelled the buried-treasure rumours."

"What did it say?" Deborah leaned towards her aunt. "Can you make anything of it?"

"Try for yourself," Louise said, and slowly recited:

*"Tourne à gauche
Tourne à droit
Quand le doigt*

Est sur le doigt
Tout est à toi.''

Slowly, Deborah translated:

"Turn to the left
Turn to the right
When the finger
Is on the finger
Everything is yours."

Her face fell. "But . . . it doesn't seem to make any sense."

"I have never been able to see anything in it," Madame d'Auray agreed. "In fact, I have always suspected that it is just one of those word games that so amused Raoul and the *vicomte.*"

"It does say 'everything is yours.'" Deborah was still frowning over the rhyme.

"But it doesn't say what 'everything' it means," Madame pointed out. "If it is a clue, which I doubt, then it is in one of their codes and I'm afraid that neither Raoul nor the *vicomte* had time to tell us about the key. No, my dear, the treasure is lost and I shall waste no more of this beautiful morning on bygone sorrows. Finish up your coffee and come up to the attics with me."

Deborah obediently lifted her coffee bowl, but paused with it halfway to her mouth. "The attics?"

Louise smiled mischievously. "Yes, my dear. There are chestfuls of old fabrics and gowns up there—some of them from my Paris and London days. There's an excellent seamstress in the village. So come along, Debs. Between us, I think we may contrive a respectable wardrobe for you. I believe we may consign that puce-coloured gown to the rubbish heap."

WHILE DEBORAH RUMMAGED delightedly amid silks and cambrics, Lord Crichton idled away the time outdoors. He sat in a comfortable wooden chair with his leg on a small footstool. He was at the back of the house on the first terrace.

A set of ancient stone stairs led down to a broader terrace, lined on two sides by brown stone outbuildings with elaborate slate tile roofs. A dolphin-shaped fountain was playing in the middle of the lower lawn. Outside one of the stone sheds a maid was grooming a large white goat.

It must be a Kashmir, Lord Crichton thought as he watched the combings being carefully transferred to a basket. He chuckled a little at the goat's expression of long-suffering condescension. Then he took another sip of the cool blackberry cordial in front of him.

Really, it was very pleasant here. It was delightful that France was once again accessible to English travellers. He remembered what Freddie had said about the de Keroualles. But of course Gwendolyn could not yet have arrived. Certainly he would not thrust himself into her reunion with her friends. No, in a few days perhaps he might send a letter, arrange a meeting. . . . There was no hurry, really. . . .

Lazily, Lord Crichton watched a woman come round the corner of the house. He wondered who it might be. Then she stopped for a moment to touch a magnificent crimson rose. There could be no mistaking those hands. He stiffened as Deborah Stormont approached.

"Please, Lord Crichton, do not get up," she said anxiously as he reached for the stick leaning against the chair. "You must not disturb your leg."

"Thank you, Miss Stormont. Will you not be seated?" He looked narrowly at her. She looked decidedly different this morning. Ah! He had it! She'd done something to her hair. It wasn't scraped back into that ugly roll; it was piled on top of her head, with long ringlets tumbling becomingly down.

And the dress: it was nothing like those dark, shapeless things she'd worn before. This was a pretty blue with a white ribbon sash.

"After all," Madame d'Auray had said, "as it was made for me, it will naturally be a trifle short for you. But here are a pair of lace-trimmed pantalons which will take care of that, *ma chère.*"

Though Lord Crichton was vaguely aware that the gown was outmoded, he thought that the change in her appearance improved Miss Stormont enormously. Curiously, however, this change did not warm his feelings towards her. She might look different, he thought, but she was still the same stiff female.

Witness, for example, the cold, formal voice in which she enquired after his health. Forgetting his pleasure of a few minutes earlier, Lord Crichton thought bitterly that if it weren't for this woman, he would be up in Scotland, enjoying some fine shooting. He answered her in the same cool tones. "I am much better, Miss Stormont. I believe that my leg will sustain no lasting injury from the, er, accident."

At the ironic inflection in the last word, Deborah clenched her hands tighter together under the table. How she hated that tone! But she forced herself to speak evenly. "I am afraid that I must tender you my apologies, again, my lord. The accident was entirely due to my carelessness and I must beg your forgiveness."

"Certainly, Miss Stormont." Lord Crichton's glance wandered to where the Duchesse had tired of being groomed. Angrily twitching her long ears, she skipped away from the maid and went to drink daintily from the fountain bowl. "Pray think no more of it."

Deborah's nails were digging into her palms. He could hardly have made his lack of interest plainer. On the road she had begun to think that they might be able to rub along together—he had certainly understood her nervousness about meeting Tante Louise again. But now . . .

However, Deborah told herself, it was scarcely to be wondered at if he had taken her in dislike. After all, she had caused him to postpone his proposal of marriage; she had hauled him off to France and then tumbled him down a mounting block onto his weak leg. So now she must do whatever she could to remedy matters.

"Lord Crichton," she began again and saw his long mouth twitch in unconscious irritation. "My brother tells me that we have inadvertently caused you to postpone an—" she met those cool grey eyes and flushed a little "—an important, er, personal matter."

"It is of no consequence, Miss Stormont." Beron's tone was icy. "You could not have known. Pray say no more about it."

"But I can do something about it now," Deborah said eagerly. "My aunt informs me that the Vicomtesse de Keroualles, with whom I understand your fiancée—"

"She is not yet my fiancée, Miss Stormont."

"Oh! Your intended fiancée, then. I collect she is to stay with the de Keroualles. My aunt says the château is but a twenty-minute ride away. I shall send a message to inform the young lady—"

"That is not necessary, Miss Stormont." Beron's eyes were cold and his mouth had narrowed to a thin line.

Deborah stopped for a moment, but she did not heed these danger signs. She was bent on making some arrangement, any arrangement that would compensate for the trouble she had caused him. "No? Perhaps you are right, my lord. A message is not the thing. It is news which should be passed on in person, for undoubtedly your fiancée... the young lady will be much disturbed to hear of your mishap."

Beron tried to interrupt, but Deborah rushed on. "Yes, I do agree with you. I shall go there myself, then I shall be able to reassure her that you are recovering and that she need not disturb herself. I'm sure my aunt will provide a carriage, so I shall just—"

"Miss Stormont!" Beron had grasped his stick and pulled himself upright. His eyes glittered and an angry flush stained his cheeks. "You will do nothing of the sort. Nothing! Do you understand me? Nothing!"

"B-b-but," Deborah stammered, "I was only trying to help—"

"Rid yourself of the notion, Miss Stormont, that I require your help."

"Oh!" Deborah's face was as pale as his lordship's was red. "Oh!"

"Yes, Miss Stormont, difficult as it may be for you to believe, I am quite capable of managing my own affairs. I shall communicate with my fianc—" he ground his teeth "—with my intended fiancée, as and when I decide. You," he continued, his burning gaze sweeping over her, *"you* may content yourself with directing your brother's life and the life of anyone else foolish enough to permit such interference. But I will not!" His fist clenched on the stick. "I trust I make myself clear?"

"Very clear, my lord." Deborah held herself very tall. "I beg your pardon, my lord." She nodded coldly at him and moved as calmly as she could to the French doors. It was only when they closed behind her that she began to run, and it was only when she reached the sanctuary of her own room that she burst at last into tears.

CHAPTER NINE

IN A SMALL PARTY in a remote country house it is difficult
for two people to avoid each other. Both Miss Stormont
and Lord Crichton were angry and both thought that they
did well to be angry. Politeness and good breeding demanded that they not display their private feelings in public. They were obliged, therefore, to meet each other and
to treat each other with at least the semblance of courtesy.

Naturally Peregrine noticed nothing amiss. He had been
somewhat cast down by Freddie's departure, but the story
of the treasure had plucked him up no end. He had spent
hours tapping walls, measuring panels, peering up chim-
neys, moving furniture and generally getting in the way of
the domestic staff.

Madame d'Auray was not so unperceptive, but she kept
her own counsel, merely filling in any awkward pauses and
arranging that Deborah and Beron should have frequent
occasion for brief private conversation. By the third day,
these tactics had produced a considerable thaw in the frigid
propriety with which they treated each other.

Mr. Wimpole had returned that morning and found
nothing remarkable in their relationship. But he was relieved to discover that he himself had come swiftly on the
heels of the long-awaited Eccles.

That worthy had professed himself deeply shocked at
the sight of his master in borrowed clothes. Never, he declared hoarsely, had he thought to see his lordship in a coat

which *strained across the shoulders*. He remedied that as soon as possible and began putting his mark on his lordship's bedroom.

"Jolly good thing he's arrived," said Freddie, eyeing the coat of blue Bath superfine that Beron was now sporting. "Don't mind your using my stuff, old fellow, but that coat's much more the thing."

"Thank you, Freddie. It feels much better. I lived in constant dread of hearing yours split straight down my spine." Beron smiled. He felt much more at ease in his own clothes and also, he thought, with a fresh supply of his own funds.

"What did you make of these de Keroualles?" Freddie asked casually, as they went downstairs.

Lord Crichton paused to smooth a wrinkle from his sleeve. "De Keroualles, Freddie? I have not wished to intrude too soon upon Miss Phipps-Hedder's reunion with her friends."

"Too soon?" Mr. Wimpole blinked at his friend. Surely Gwendolyn should be well settled in by now? If Beron's intent was to present himself as the impatient lover, anxious to overcome any misunderstanding, then this delay would not help his cause.

"I'm sure Gwendolyn will be delighted to see you, old chap," he ventured. "Must be wonderin' what happened to you—if you've changed your mind or what, don't you know."

"Ah, yes, Freddie, but she is a sensible girl. I'm sure she won't refine too much upon such a trifle."

Freddie was somewhat taken aback by this description of Gwendolyn. But before he could comment, Beron had shepherded him out onto the terrace where the rest of the party were sitting. After greeting the others, Freddie turned to a much more pressing concern.

"Remember that Muscadet?" he asked.

"Have you found it, Freddie?" Perry demanded eagerly.

"No, but—" Freddie leaned forward "—I've got a clue!"

Beron's mouth quirked upwards at one corner. Miss Stormont watched it in fascination.

"Well, tell us, then!" Perry urged.

"I've heard of a small vineyard, some miles to the south. There's an inn attached and I've heard the landlord has some noteworthy vintages."

"That doesn't seem a lot to go on."

Freddie looked suspiciously around, hitched his chair closer and lowered his voice. "My aunt's butler heard an Englishman's been travelling the neighbourhood. Asking all sorts of questions, the butler says. Now I ask you," Freddie said portentously, "what else could he be after?"

Remarkably, both Miss Stormont and Lord Crichton were afflicted with a fit of coughing at the same time. Freddie glanced at them, then he jerked, shouted and leapt up, knocking over his chair.

"Here!" he yelled. "What's all this?"

They all stared.

There was the sound of cloth tearing as Freddie whirled round and pointed a trembling finger.

The Duchesse stood before him, her long, narrow head tilted aristocratically to one side. From either side of her mouth trailed the two long tails of Freddie's dark green coat. A beatific expression crossed the goat's face, she swallowed, and the coattails disappeared.

"Here," gasped Freddie. "Nugee made that coat!" He took a step towards the goat. Immediately the gold eyes narrowed, the long ears went back. The Duchesse lowered her head and Freddie glimpsed twin curved silvered horns. He stepped hurriedly backwards.

"My dear Mr. Wimpole." Madame d'Auray's voice trembled, but she endeavoured to infuse it with proper concern. "I am so sorry. Pray sit down and let me give you another cider."

Freddie eyed the Duchesse, who was still meditatively chewing. He edged his chair to one side and inched himself into it. "That goat ate my coat," he said, almost as if unable to believe what had just occurred.

"Deplorable," soothed his hostess, pushing a plate of *biscuits de Nantes* towards him. "I'm afraid we should keep that animal tethered. She is most undiscriminating in her tastes."

"Wouldn't say that," replied Freddie dispiritedly. "In fact, dashed discriminating of her to choose a coat by Nugee!"

"Never mind, Freddie." Lord Crichton's own voice was none too steady. "I shall stand you a new one when we return to London, and for now you may change into one of those you so kindly lent me."

"Hi, Freddie, look to your cider!" Perry shouted.

Freddie had put his china tankard on the wide arm of his chair. Now he turned and his eyes bulged.

The Duchesse was standing beside him, her nose buried in the tankard. Her eyes were tightly shut and she was steadily lapping up his drink.

"Oh, dear!" Madame d'Auray jumped up and waved frantically at one of the maids crossing the lower terrace. After a rapid exchange of French, the girl grinned and hurried up the stairs. She grasped the goat and tugged her off. The Duchesse's indignant bleats faded as she was relentlessly removed and tethered behind the farthest outbuilding.

The party applied themselves to restoring Freddie's equanimity. And, at last, clad in a fresh coat, he and Perry set out on the trail of the Muscadet.

Deborah took her sketch-book and wandered down the steps. She followed a path behind the stone barns and came across the Duchesse reclining beneath a gooseberry bush and chewing her cud. The goat did not deign to acknowledge her greeting, so Deborah passed on through another stand of the poplars which gave Le Bois qui Chante its name.

On the other side, she crossed a wide meadow and came upon a large pond. A couple of willows dipped gracefully over the water and there were clumps of marguerites and goldenrod. Green, saucer-shaped lily pads, dotted here and there with their spears of white flowers, floated on the water.

Deborah found a grassy hillock and sat down. It had been rather a long time since she'd held a pencil, she thought, flexing her long fingers. It was good to get back to work.

She stared intently at the scene for a few moments, then began to draw. She worked steadily for some time, and only reluctantly stopped to stretch her hand and fingers.

"Good afternoon, Miss Stormont. Do I disturb you?"

Deborah spun round. "Lord Crichton!"

His lordship sat down on the grass near her and clasped his hands about his bent knees. He seemed perfectly content to admire the view and to remain silent.

But Deborah saw that he was no longer using a stick. "Your leg is quite recovered, my lord?"

"Yes, indeed. The doctor has just been and pronounced me fit. I may even ride if I wish."

"Then you will be leaving the Bois soon?" Deborah kept her eyes on her sketch-book.

"I expect so," said Beron vaguely. "But your aunt has invited me to remain as long as I wish."

Deborah doodled restlessly on the corner of the page. Then she thought: of course he won't go to the countess. He'll go to the de Keroualles. But after their last interview on that subject, she had no intention of mentioning her conclusions.

There was silence again. It was not uncomfortable, though Deborah was aware of Lord Crichton's presence. He, however, seemed to be intent on the scenery, on the whirring of crickets and the gentle sighing of the distant poplars.

"Are you sketching the *étang,* Miss Stormont?" he asked at length.

"*Étang?*"

"Your aunt was telling me about it. Medieval monks created many of these ponds to provide fish for the poor of the parish to eat."

"I did not know that," said Deborah, looking at the pond with new interest.

"But you found it interesting enough to sketch, none-theless?" he asked again.

"N-not exactly," Deborah said rather hesitantly.

Lord Crichton smiled rather indulgently. Sketching was a genteel occupation for females, but that did not mean they all had a natural aptitude for it. Miss Stormont must be embarrassed by her amateur efforts. Intending to offer some reassuring words, he rose and strolled over to her. But when he saw Deborah's work, he stood stock-still. He had expected to see the usual conventional representation of a rather conventional scene. But Deborah had not sketched the panorama at all.

She had chosen what looked like a bush of huge wild rhubarb, with thick brownish stems. As he gazed at the clear, incisive strokes, the precise detail, the control and confidence in every line, Lord Crichton began to feel particularly foolish. Mentally castigating himself for his complacency, Beron said humbly, "You are an accomplished artist, Miss Stormont."

Deborah looked quickly at him, but he seemed perfectly sincere. She blushed a little at his praise. "I have always preferred to do plants, rather than landscape," she said.

"There can be no doubt you do them well," he replied respectfully.

"Do you like the hogweed, then?"

"Is that what you call this rhubarb stuff? You've certainly captured its sinister aspect. One can almost count the thorns on those stems."

"I've seen it along the river in Salisbury, but never this size."

"I shall take care to avoid it here," Beron said. "It would be monstrously uncomfortable to fall into the clutches of such a plant." He looked down at her. "Are you determined to sketch all afternoon, Miss Stormont, or would you care to walk on a little with me?"

"Why no, I mean, yes!" Flustered by the invitation, Deborah scrambled to her feet, dropping her sketch-book and pencils.

As they both reached for them, their hands touched. Deborah snatched hers back as if it had been scalded. But Lord Crichton stood up, and fitting the pencils back into their box, he said easily, "I should have known those were artist's hands, Miss Stormont."

"Where did you wish to walk, my lord?" Unable to deal with the compliment, Deborah tried to turn the subject. She took the pencil box and stuffed it and the sketch-book into her satchel. Lord Crichton offered to carry it, but she shook her head and slung it over one shoulder.

They circled the pond and set off along a rather overgrown path.

"Your aunt, as I said, has been discussing the attractions of the area. Down here, she tells me there is a field of menhirs."

"Megaliths?" Deborah stopped. "Do you mean, like those at Stonehenge?"

"Not exactly, I think. This is, I collect, an alignment. The great stones are arranged in lines; *allées*, the French call them."

"I should certainly like to see them!" Deborah exclaimed. "I have been so busy settling in that I have not much discussed the area with my aunt. But I had no idea that such monuments were also found in France."

"According to Madame d'Auray, there are many such erections in Brittany."

The path had now led them into a pine wood and the branches edged out over the walkway. They had to walk in single file so there was little chance of further conversation.

As he pushed through the branches, holding them till Deborah had passed, Lord Crichton reflected that she was the most disconcerting female he had ever met. Just when he thought he understood her, she showed another facet of her personality and set him all about again.

Behind him, Miss Stormont's mind was running on much the same lines. What a volatile creature his lordship must be, thought Deborah as she let the branches snap back behind her. They had had that withering scene on the terrace. For two days he'd treated her with frozen civility, and yet now he was praising her drawing and actually asking for her company. She shook her head as they emerged from the wood and stood blinking at the sun.

They were standing beneath a huge old pine, whose straight trunk reached at least ten feet overhead before branching out in dark green needles.

"This must be the field," said Beron, gesturing.

At first, Deborah's impression was of a chaotic jumble of rocks. But gradually, she discerned five distinct rows. Not all the stones were standing. Time and the elements had worked on them. Presumably they all once had been pillar-shaped, but now some were sculpted into fans and wedges; others had cracked and broken; still others lay flat on the ground. Most strange of all were the few which neither time nor weather seemed to have touched. From where she stood, Deborah could see one enormous menhir that appeared as tall and as straight as when it had first been raised all those thousands of years ago.

"Shall we go closer?" Lord Crichton held out an arm.

Deborah hesitated a moment. But the ground did seem uneven and she did not wish to appear rude.

"Thank you, my lord," she said, placing her long fingers lightly on his arm as they moved out among the stones.

After a moment, she took a deep breath. "Do you feel it, my lord? I have felt exactly the same thing at home at Stonehenge and Avebury." She was going to go on, but she suddenly stopped. Perhaps Lord Crichton would think she was being unduly fanciful.

His lordship was surveying the field. "I know exactly what you mean, Miss Stormont. An aura of incalculable age and, I think, a sense of impenetrable mystery."

"Yes," Deborah breathed. "I wonder if we shall ever know just why these stone formations were made."

Lord Crichton shook his head. "I have read many explanations of the English ones, Miss Stormont, ranging from religious ceremonies to astronomical observations. I do not know that I find any totally persuasive." He ran his hand thoughtfully over the nearest menhir. "Whatever the reason, it must have been of consuming importance to those who undertook the massive effort."

They walked on in silence for a while, both busy with their own thoughts. Then Beron smiled at her.

"Well, Miss Stormont, these are not plants, but do you care to sketch them nonetheless? I am in no haste and should be pleased to await your pleasure."

"The shapes are certainly intriguing," Deborah said, looking about. "It would be a challenge, though, to reproduce that patina in pencil. Perhaps I shall try, after all."

They found some large rocks at the edge of the field and Deborah settled herself on one of these, her back resting against another more upright one. Lord Crichton stretched out in the grass beside her, his hands behind his head.

At first Deborah found it difficult to draw in his presence. But, gradually, the work absorbed her and she forgot everything else, her attention centred on trying to capture the texture which mosses, lichen and age had all contributed to the stones' surfaces.

Lord Crichton looked up into the clear blue sky, and let his thoughts wander at will. It was, he supposed, time to do something about Gwendolyn. Presumably, she had had time to settle in by now. As Freddie had indicated, he shouldn't let things go any further. He had the grace to admit that his inaction had been at least partially caused by his anger with Deborah Stormont. Because she had wanted him to act, he had refused to do so. But, he must own, that was a childish way to demonstrate his independence.

He let his eyes slide towards Miss Stormont. There could be no doubt that her new hair-style suited her, softened her somewhat severe expression. The apple green colour she was wearing today lent a glow to her complexion.

She seemed much more relaxed of late, younger and less forbidding. He watched the long white fingers move elegantly and surely over the paper.

Miss Stormont appeared oblivious to his scrutiny. But suddenly her hands stopped, and she lifted her head as if to listen. She turned to him.

"My lord, I think we are not alone."

Beron raised himself on one elbow. Then he, too, heard voices. He stood up. "I suppose it is not unlikely that others have come to see the menhirs," he said casually, but nonetheless he moved closer to her and let his hand fall gently to her shoulder.

"Look!" Deborah pointed.

A group of young people had come into view on the other side of the field. There was a young man, dark-haired, and an equally dark girl. The other girl was brown-haired and, as they came closer, she ran a little ahead of the others. None of them had seen the two by the rocks.

The brown-haired girl stopped and turned laughingly back to her companions. Deborah felt Beron stiffen and his hand fell away. As he strode out into the field, the brown-haired girl turned back and saw him. She grew suddenly pale, her hand flew to her breast, she staggered and would have fallen to the ground if the dark-haired young man had not rushed forward and caught her in his arms.

CHAPTER TEN

DEBORAH SCRAMBLED UP and ran over to the others. They looked, she thought, like actors, frozen in a tableau. She pushed past Beron and spoke to the young man holding the girl.

"Pray lay her down on the grass over there, *monsieur.* There is a small stream, I see, and we may bathe her face."

Her voice apparently broke the spell. Without a word, Lord Crichton strode off towards the water.

"*Mais oui!*" the dark-haired girl cried. "*Dépêche-toi, Edouard! Ici, vite!*"

Gently the young man laid the girl down in the grass. Lord Crichton returned and silently handed his damp handkerchief to Deborah. She took the girl's head in her lap and began to cool her forehead.

The French girl dropped down beside them and began to chafe her friend's hand. "*Comment vas-tu, ma chère?*" she asked coaxingly. "*Ouvres tes yeux, je te prie,* Gwendolyn."

The girl called Gwendolyn moaned and turned her head. Her eyelids fluttered and she opened large brown eyes.

"Where am I?" she asked in English, passing a hand over her eyes. "I thought I..."

"*Ah, bon!*" The other girl sighed in relief and sat back on her heels. "You are better, Gwendolyn."

Gwendolyn struggled to sit up and Deborah supported her for a moment. "I made sure I saw..." she repeated.

ACCEPT FOUR BRAND-NEW

YOURS

We'd like to send you four free Harlequin novels, worth more than $11.00, to introduce you to the benefits of the Harlequin Reader Service®. We hope your free books will convince you to subscribe, but that's up to you. Accepting them places you under no obligation to buy anything, but we hope you'll want to continue with the Reader Service.

So unless we hear from you, every other month, we'll send you 4 additional Harlequin Regency Romance™ novels to read and enjoy. If you choose to keep them, you'll pay just $2.69* per volume—a saving of 30¢ each off the cover price. There is no charge for shipping and handling. There are no hidden extras! And you may cancel at any time, for any reason, just by sending us a note or a shipping statement marked "cancel." You can even return any shipment to us at our expense. Either way, the free books and gifts are yours to keep!

ALSO FREE!
VICTORIAN PICTURE FRAME

This lovely Victorian pewter-finish miniature is perfect for displaying a treasured photograph—and it's yours *absolutely free*—when you accept our no-risk offer.

Perfect for a treasured Photograph

Plus a FREE mystery Gift! follow instructions at right.

*Terms and prices subject to change without notice.
Sales taxes applicable in NY.

© 1990 Harlequin Enterprises Limited

WE EVEN PROVIDE FREE POSTAGE!

It costs you *nothing* to send for your free books — we've paid the postage on the attached reply card. And we'll pick up the postage on your shipment of free books and gifts, and also on any subsequent shipments of books, should you choose to become a subscriber. Unlike many book clubs, we charge *nothing* for postage and handling!

DETACH AND RETURN TODAY

"You did, Miss Phipps-Hedder." Lord Crichton came forward. "You did see me. You were not expecting to encounter me in France and I most abjectly beg pardon for announcing my presence in such a hurly-burly fashion."

The girl closed her eyes again. "But... but... Papa said... I mean I thought—"

"I had intended to write to you, Miss Phipps-Hedder. Believe me, it was not my purpose to startle you in any way."

The dark young man standing to one side shifted his feet and muttered to himself in French. The French girl glanced swiftly at him, then rose to her feet in one graceful movement. She had a lively pixie face, framed by tight black curls and dominated by a pair of dancing black eyes. She bestowed a dazzling smile on Deborah and Beron.

"*Mademoiselle, monsieur,* permit me to introduce myself," she said in prettily accented English. "I am Julie de Keroualle and this is my brother Edouard, *le vicomte.*" She laughed mischievously up at Lord Crichton. "You at least are already acquainted with our friend, *monsieur.*" She turned to Deborah. "Are you also a friend of Gwendolyn's, *mademoiselle?*"

Wordlessly, Deborah shook her head. She heard Lord Crichton introduce both her and himself, but her gaze was on the brown-haired girl, still leaning for support on her arm. So this was the girl to whom Beron was hastening off to propose when she and Perry had so unceremoniously detained him.

She had a great deal of countenance, Deborah was forced to admit, but, well, wasn't it a trifle poor-spirited of her to swoon like that? Deborah shook herself. She must not be uncharitable and, after all, wasn't it said that gentlemen preferred women of sensibility? Deborah thought a little wistfully that she herself would never have fainted in such a situation.

Miss Phipps-Hedder was still having trouble understanding Beron's presence. "But my lord—" she frowned up at him "—you are in France. How did—"

Lord Crichton's ironic glance flickered over Deborah. Unconsciously she raised her chin and stared back at him.

"An unforeseen contingency required me to undertake an ... er, unexpected journey," Beron said blandly, not taking his eyes from Deborah. "I sent a letter to your father, Miss Phipps-Hedder, but no doubt you had left before it arrived."

"Oh!" Gwendolyn staggered to her feet. "So Papa did not, that is, you came on business of your own?"

Beron's eyebrows rose and he turned to look at her. "When I last spoke to your father, Miss Phipps-Hedder, I was not, er, contemplating a visit to France."

A little colour had come back to Gwendolyn's face. She held out a hand. "I'm afraid I didn't catch your name, but I do thank you so much, Miss—"

"Stormont," Deborah supplied. "I am glad to see you better."

"I am sorry I behaved like such a pea-goose." Her colour deepened a little as she turned to Beron. "Pray forgive me, my lord. You did startle me, but I hope you will forgive my silliness."

"Certainly." Beron took her hand and bowed over it. "My clumsiness was entirely to blame." He spoke to Julie de Keroualle. "I am delighted to meet you, *mademoiselle,* and you also, *Monsieur le Vicomte.*"

For a moment Deborah thought that the young man was going to refuse Beron's hand. But he shook it quickly and mumbled *"Enchanté"* without a lifting of his scowl.

Julie de Keroualle was talking quietly to her friend.

"Gwendolyn is still feeling a little unwell," she said. "So, if you please, my lord Crichton," she added, putting the accent on the last syllable, "I think we should go home now."

"Certainement." Edouard stepped protectively to Gwendolyn's other side. *"Il faut qu'elle se repose immediatement."*

"Without doubt," Lord Crichton agreed. "You have had a shock, Miss Phipps-Hedder, and quiet will be the best thing for you. Shall we escort you home?"

"Oh, no!" Gwendolyn said. "I mean, Edouard, that is, the *vicomte* drove us here in the tilbury. It is just the other side of the meadow."

"Very well, then," Beron replied. "I shall do myself the honour of calling upon you in the next few days."

The others said their farewells and he and Deborah stood watching while the three crossed the meadow and vanished behind a line of thorn trees.

"Are you finished with your sketching, Miss Stormont, or do you prefer to continue?"

"No, my lord," said Deborah quietly. "I should like to go home now." She went to gather up her things. It had not been, she reflected, an auspicious reunion for a man and his intended fiancée. She did not wonder that his lordship was not in a talkative mood and she said nothing at all to break the silence as they walked homeward.

When they came round the stone barns however, Lord Crichton gave a shout of laughter and pointed up to the first terrace.

Madame d'Auray, Freddie and Perry were all standing before one of the willow tables. They were staring solemnly at a large brown bottle in the centre of the table. Louise's crochet-work lay discarded on a chair. From the corner of the house, the Duchesse too had fixed her amber eyes on the bottle.

Deborah giggled. "Do you think it can be the Muscadet?"

"Not in a brown bottle," said his lordship cheerfully. "But let's go on and see, shall we?"

As they came up the steps, Freddie saw them. "Just in time!" he exclaimed. "Come and taste this!"

"What is it?" Beron asked, regarding the rather squat bottle.

"It's a Banyuls!" declared Freddie impressively.

Lord Crichton twitched an eyebrow at Deborah. "Well, we shall plead guilty, Freddie. We do not know what a Banyuls may be."

"It's extremely rare," Perry put in. "Freddie says we were dashed lucky to come across it."

"Don't see it much in England," Freddie said, motioning them to chairs. "It's a kind of French fortified wine—in the sherry or port family. Madame d'Auray has sent for some glasses and figs, just the thing for an afternoon snack."

Deborah had been rather hoping for a cup of tea, but she suppressed the thought and watched with interest as Bigard placed a silver tray, glasses and a silver bottle-opener on the table. With great ceremony, the butler picked up the opener and presented it to Freddie.

Perry drew in his breath and leaned forward. Glancing sideways at Lord Crichton, Debs could see the tiny muscle working at the corner of his mouth. She could feel another giggle building, so she told herself firmly to behave and gave her full attention to Freddie.

Slowly, with due reverence, Mr. Wimpole lifted the bottle, and in one practised movement, inserted the cork-pull, twisted his wrist and removed the cork. Gravely he passed the bottle to Perry, who sniffed it deeply with his eyes closed. Freddie repossessed the bottle and poured the deep brown liquid into the glasses.

To Deborah it looked like sherry in colour and when she gingerly tasted it, it had a rich, almost nutty flavour.

"Reminds me of an Amontillado," said Louise, holding up her glass so that the sunlight broke into a thousand facets of gold and brown.

"So that's where Perry gets his talent," Freddie beamed at her. "It's made in much the same process." He nodded at Perry. "You can distinguish the raisin taste of course, but there are more subtle notes of black currant and chocolate."

"Chocolate?" Rather dubiously, Perry sipped again, and let the liquid lie on his tongue before swallowing it with a ferocious frown.

"Well, Miss Stormont?" Beron asked. "What do you make of this find?"

Deborah laughed. "I can't taste any black currant and certainly no chocolate. I am enjoying it, especially with these fi—" She was going to continue but Lord Crichton's hand fell gently on her wrist and he nodded towards Freddie.

The better to enjoy his discovery, Mr. Wimpole had lain back in his chair, his eyes closed, his glass clasped to his chest. Made curious by all the activity, the Duchesse had drawn closer. She stood behind Freddie, her head raised.

She looked, Deborah thought, rather like an aristocratic dowager who had chanced on an orgy in the butler's pantry. Now she leaned forward, her long ears brushing against Freddie's cheek. Mr. Wimpole raised a languid hand to push them away.

His fingers touched the curving horns. Freddie shouted and leapt to his feet. The wine spilled over his cream-and-crimson waistcoat. Freddie stared at the spreading stain.

"M-m-m-my new waistcoat," he choked.

Madame d'Auray jumped up and began dabbing at him with her napkin. "Pray do not worry, Freddie, my dear. I know an infallible method to remove such stains. I—"

"Ahem!" Bigard had returned. "*Madame,*" he said, paying no attention to the upheaval about him. "A gentleman has called. He has asked to speak to Mademoiselle Stormont." He bowed to Deborah.

Deborah was becoming used to Bigard's speech and had caught most of this. "To me? But I don't know anyone in France."

Bigard coughed again. "*Monsieur est anglais, je crois.*"

"English!" Perry repeated. "Goodness, Debs, is this some secret beau come to follow after you?"

"Really, Perry!" Deborah took the card Bigard was holding out to her. "Dr. Simon Trewin," she read. "Fellow, Magdalen College, Oxford." Beside her, Lord Crichton made a sudden movement, but when she turned to look at him, he offered no remark.

"Well, my dear?" Madame d'Auray said. "Would you like me to go with you to see him, or would you prefer Bigard to bring him out here?"

"I've no idea who he is," Debs replied, laying down the card, "and I cannot imagine what he should want with me."

"Then," Louise said in her placid way, "we had best have him in and find out. And, Bigard," she added in lowered tones, "please see that the Duchesse is removed."

Momentarily foiled, the goat stood a little back from Freddie, tossing her head and eyeing him speculatively.

"Dashed animal is determined to consume my wardrobe," Freddie muttered, and did not turn back to the table till goat and butler had vanished round the side of the house.

"Come on," Perry said, "I'll go up with you while you change. These scholarly chaps aren't my cup of tea at all."

Deborah thought Lord Crichton might also take this opportunity to withdraw, but he made no move. His eyes were fixed on the square of pasteboard Debs had put down by her glass. She could not see the expression in them.

"Monsieur Simon Trewin," announced Bigard, pronouncing the name in the French way.

A tall, strongly built man strode forward. He had light brown hair and was well, if rather severely, dressed. He made his bow before Tante Louise. "Madame d'Auray," he said.

Louis gave him her hand. "May I introduce my niece, Miss Stormont, and our guest, Lord Crichton?"

The newcomer shook hands with Deborah and Beron, then sat down in the chair Louise had indicated. "I must apologize for interrupting your holiday, Miss Stormont," he said, "but I had no idea that you were leaving England and I also had no idea when you might return, so I have ventured to approach you here. I must hope you will forgive my presumption."

"It must have been rather taxing to, er, discover Miss Stormont's direction." Lord Crichton's voice was at its lowest but Deborah glanced up sharply at its tone.

Trewin laughed ruefully. "Oh, it was, it was. But judge of my disappointment when I finally arrived on your doorstep in Salisbury, only to hear that you had already departed for France."

"But you were not dismayed by this intelligence?" Crichton's tone had not altered.

Smilingly Trewin shook his head. "I was at a stand for a while, I must own. But then I happened upon the vicar of your parish, Miss Stormont, and he told me that you were to visit a relative near Redon."

"A most fortunate encounter," Beron murmured.

Deborah had listened rather impatiently to all this. "But what I do not understand is why you should have wanted to contact me at all, sir."

Simon Trewin smiled understandingly at her. "I may answer that in two words: Professor Chudwith."

"Professor Chudwith?" Deborah echoed.

"Yes, don't you remember, Miss Stormont? He bought two of your plant studies in Salisbury some months ago."

"I do remember, of course, but what has—"

"Let me explain, if you will. I am a colleague, a very junior one, I hasten to add, of the professor's. He showed me your drawings and they were exactly what I wanted."

Deborah spread her hands in an eloquent gesture of confusion. "I still don't..."

"I am in the process of preparing a book, Miss Stormont. A guide, I should say, to the native flora of the British Isles." He smiled a little deprecatingly. "I know such guides exist, but many of them are outdated and I have ambitions, Miss Stormont. I mean to do the most comprehensive, most up-to-date guide possible."

"Admirable," Lord Crichton murmured, "perfectly admirable."

Deborah frowned at him and then said, "Do you mean, Dr. Trewin, that you wish to ask me to—"

"To do the illustrations for my book? Yes indeed, Miss Stormont, that is what I have come all this way to discuss with you." He held up his hand. "I know it will come as a surprise to you and it is something that many ladies might hesitate over, so I beg you will make no decision yet. I shall give you more details later and answer whatever questions you may have. In the meantime," he added, rising, "I am sure you will wish to discuss the whole matter with your family."

"My niece will naturally do so." Madame d'Auray rose also. "But will you stay for some refreshment, Dr. Trewin? Or are you perhaps in mid-journey?"

"Thank you, Madam." Trewin sat down again. "I am staying at an inn in the next village. I have begun a study of some local ferns, so I stay to complete that."

"Then I trust we shall have the pleasure of welcoming you to the Bois again in the near future." Louise tinkled the little brass bell by her side.

Simon Trewin proved a pleasant companion and an easy conversationalist. Which was just as well, Deborah thought, eyeing his lordship in disapproval. Beron was reclining elegantly in his chair, an air of casual interest surrounding him. He spoke only occasionally and then in what Debs considered an odiously sardonic manner.

After a correct period of time, Simon Trewin pushed back his chair. Punctiliously he thanked Madame d'Auray for her hospitality, bowed to Deborah and promised they would speak again soon. He took an equally correct leave of Lord Crichton, ignoring the latter's provocative "Not *adieu,* I think, but rather *au revoir.*"

Madame d'Auray walked along the terrace with him. She stopped halfway to point out some late-blooming Gloire de Dijon roses.

Beside her, Deborah heard Lord Crichton chuckle. "Are you impressed by your scholarly visitor, Miss Stormont?"

"Dr. Trewin appears to be a perfect gentleman," Deborah said repressively.

Lord Crichton remained amused. "But others at the Bois do not appear to share your opinion." He looked towards her aunt and the visitor.

The Duchesse had escaped Bigard's surveillance. She crept up behind Simon Trewin as he studied the roses. She was directly behind him now, delicately pawing the ground with one hoof. She bent her head.

Unfortunately, Trewin chose that very moment to bend over to sniff a particularly fine specimen. Deborah gasped and stood up. "Dr. Trewin," she called. "Watch—" But she was too late.

The Duchesse charged. Louise shrieked and Simon Trewin went sailing into the air, high over the Gloire de Dijons, and vanished below the first terrace.

"Oh, no!" Deborah raced towards her aunt, Lord Crichton sauntering after her.

Louise was leaning over a balustrade, peering anxiously down. In some trepidation, Deborah peeped over herself. The drop was not great here, but underneath was a large stone trough used to gather rainwater. The Duchesse's aim had been unerring. Dr. Trewin floundered and swore in his unexpected bath.

"I say!" Freddie and Perry had returned. One glance at the goat triumphantly munching roses, and Freddie had grasped the situation. "I say," he repeated, "has that goat got someone else?"

"Perhaps," said Lord Crichton blandly, "she also took exception to his coat, though it is not, I should have said, by Nugee."

"*Urrgh!*" shouted Simon Trewin, splashing furiously. "*Urrrgh!* Someone get me out of here!"

"By Jove," said Freddie, leaning interestedly over, "look, there's some kind of green mould in that water. See how it clings to him."

"So there is." Perry peered over his shoulder. "Ugh! Slimy stuff."

"Oh, I don't know." Lord Crichton brushed a speck of moss from his own immaculate buckskins. "He might make a study of French mould, too. It is, after all, a species of plant."

"Will you cease joking and go to help him?" Deborah demanded in exasperation.

"Help is at hand." Beron pointed down to where Bigard was advancing upon Dr. Trewin with an outspread blanket.

"I must help, too." Louise darted towards the steps.

With a last glare at the men, Deborah hurried after her.

"Should we go down, do you think?" Freddie asked as Simon Trewin was wrapped in the blanket and led away.

"I think not." Lord Crichton was scratching the Duchesse's ear. She stood entranced, her head weaving from side to side, a half-eaten Gloire de Dijon hanging from her mouth. "He is already being most adequately looked after. Besides . . ." He gestured towards the table.

"By George, yes! There's still some of the Banyuls left!" Freddie exclaimed. "Come on, Beron, come on, Perry, let's not let it go to waste."

Lord Crichton followed, but he did not sit down until he had chosen the largest and juiciest of the figs and fed it to the Duchesse of Brittany.

CHAPTER ELEVEN

SIMON TREWIN had been fussed over, dried, given fresh clothes, this time courtesy of Lord Crichton, and invited to pass the night at the Bois. During dinner he had attempted to demur, insisting that he would not wish to impose upon his hostess in such a manner.

"Of course you do not impose on me," Madame d'Auray replied. "And, you must know, Dr. Trewin, that I am entirely mortified by the behaviour of my...my pet."

Trewin had recovered his equanimity and smiled forgivingly at his hostess. "No need at all, *Madame,* I assure you. Pray forget the entire incident."

Freddie sipped blissfully at the Montrachet he had chosen for supper. "Must say, if you don't mind, Trewin, that I'm dashed glad that beast's turned her attention on you. Thought I was the only one she'd taken in dislike."

"No, Freddie, how can you think so?" Lord Crichton looked shocked. "Didn't you say her grace has a most discriminating taste?"

There was a chuckle round the table but Deborah looked sharply at him. There was something enigmatic in Beron's attitude to the young scholar. Or was it perhaps just that usual light irony that she found so baffling?

Dr. Trewin and Madame d'Auray had resumed their polite argument as to whether he should indeed spend the night there. Unexpectedly, Lord Crichton weighed in on Louise's side.

"But of course you must accept Madame d'Auray's invitation," he said in his soft voice. "You must not upset her by fleeing the scene of the, er, crime."

Deborah could see that Trewin was puzzled by his lordship. Her heart warmed to him. "Do stay, Dr. Trewin," she urged. "We should all be delighted to have you." She could feel Beron smiling in that infuriating manner, but she would not look at him. "Do stay," she repeated.

As the evening wore on, it became clear that Trewin was a distinct asset to the house party. He was an amusing and accommodating guest. He played a game of billiards with Freddie and Perry, and on his return to the salon, he partook of several hands of piquet with Deborah and her aunt.

"An agreeable young man," said Louise to her niece as they went upstairs, leaving the gentlemen to a last glass of cognac.

"Very charming," Deborah agreed. "Quite astounding that he should have come all this way simply to ask me to do some sketches."

"I don't think so," said her aunt firmly. "You must not denigrate your own talents, Debs. I am glad to see you getting some recognition at last."

Deborah laughed and kissed her aunt good-night. Deeply conscious of the responsibilities of her position, Marie-Claire was waiting for her and for a while Deborah was occupied with her preparations for bed and a discussion of what she would wear on the morrow.

But at last Marie-Claire left and Deborah climbed up the stairs to her huge bed. She lay back on the fat feather pillows, the faint scent of lavender surrounding her. She was tired, but her mind continued to race.

So many things had changed! Here they were in France and, far from being isolated, they seemed to be surrounded by people. Though now that Miss Phipps-Hedder had arrived, Lord Crichton would doubtless soon remove to the château.

Miss Stormont contemplated this thought and eventually persuaded herself that she would be relieved by his departure. How much more comfortably they would go on, she told herself, without that sardonic presence.

Then, there was Dr. Trewin—an Oxford fellow! She had to admit that his proposition was an intriguing one. It would be a responsibility and a challenge. . . .

Debs yawned and drifted into slumber.

NEXT MORNING she rose and dressed in a pretty mauve muslin, one of the village seamstresses' most successful renovations. Marie-Claire coaxed her thick hair into ringlets, piled them on top of her head and then threaded a matching mauve ribbon through them.

"Voilà, mademoiselle," she said, stepping back and allowing Deborah to admire her handiwork.

Miss Stormont stared at the figure in the pier-glass. Tentatively, she raised a hand and patted the glossy curls. "It looks, well, it looks so very young."

"Eh bien," said Marie-Claire with a laugh, "Mademoiselle is young, is she not?"

She was right, Deborah thought as she went downstairs. Twenty-three was still young.

There was no one else in the breakfast room so she ate quickly and took her bowl of café au lait out onto the terrace. Scarcely had she sat down when she saw a man coming round the outbuildings. It was Simon Trewin. He waved to her and hastened up the steps.

"Good morning, Miss Stormont. It's a beautiful day, is it not?"

"Delightful," Deborah said, waving him to a chair. "For a moment there, Dr. Trewin, I mistook you for a treasure-hunter!"

"Damn!" In drawing out his chair, Trewin had somehow managed to overturn it. He righted it, sat down and said, "I do beg your pardon, Miss Stormont. You were saying something about a hunter?"

"Treasure-hunter."

Trewin looked startled. "We are rather far from the sea, are we not? There can't be much pirate's gold about here."

Deborah laughed. "No, this is a local legend about buried treasure."

"Good morning." Aunt Louise bustled out to join them. Oddly, her handwork bag was not in her hand. Instead she held a single sheet of embossed paper. "This is a letter from the Vicomtesse de Keroualle. She writes that she understands that I have guests and invites us all to the château for lunch." She turned to Simon. "Dr. Trewin, as you are also our guest, I'm sure the invitation also includes you."

"I thank you, *madame,* but I shall not trespass further on your kindness. I must return to my inn. But, if I may, I shall return again soon to speak further of our project with Miss Stormont."

When he had taken his leave, Deborah and her aunt went in search of the others. They found Freddie and Perry attempting to race two enormous, golden brown toads across the front lawns.

Perry was less than pleased by the prospect of a visit to what he stigmatized as "some dusty old château."

"I don't know." Freddie eyed his toad. Desultorily, he poked it with a blunt stick. The creature shut its eyes and blew out its cheeks. "Not much sport in these brutes, old chap."

"I thought we might go and have another look for that wine," Perry said. "Remember, that Englishman's still nosing about."

"By George, yes!" Freddie nodded. "I meant to ask that Trewin chap if he'd heard anything of him. Let's go and catch him before he's off." He bowed to Louise and Debs. "I'll tell Beron about this invitation if you wish, *madame.*"

Madame d'Auray thanked him and hurried her niece off. After some consideration, she declared that with the addition of gloves, shawl, fan, hat and perhaps a silver locket which she would provide, Deborah's outfit would be ideal for lunch at the château.

"For, you know, the *vicomtesse* is not at all stand-offish. After all—" Louise smiled a little sadly "—she has had the same problems as I."

"Do you know her well—and her children?"

"We have known each other a long time, and of course we were both in exile in England. They were in Oxford though, so I did not see much of them. As to the children, Edouard has taken the fall in the family fortunes hard, but Julie is a delightful, merry-hearted child. But come along, Debs—we have not time to chatter if we are to be ready for lunch."

The Château de Keroualle was quite a different proposition from the Bois. It was at least twice as large, with two turreted wings on each side and an imposing front entrance, marked by a huge carved and painted coat of arms.

They were shown into a rather cavernous salon. Outside, it was still bright and warm, but there was a definite chill in this enormous, gloomy room.

Deborah studied its faded elegance. The vast expanses of velvet draperies had rubbed flat in places and there were threadbare patches in the Oriental carpet. On the silk walls there were lighter-coloured places, where Deborah imagined pictures had once hung. The furniture, while beautiful, was sparse. She shivered, finding the whole atmosphere rather dismal.

But nothing could dull Julie de Keroualle's spirits. She danced up to Madame d'Auray and kissed her, then clasped Debs's hand as she performed the introductions. The *vicomtesse* was a quiet, dignified woman who welcomed them in excellent English. As the party disposed themselves about the room, Deborah saw that Beron was attempting to guide Miss Phipps-Hedder to the confidante. However, Gwendolyn insisted that he and Mr. Wimpole sit there, while she perched on a little stool across from them.

But at lunch, his lordship's luck improved, for Miss Phipps-Hedder was seated at his right. Nonetheless, conversation was general and he had no opportunity for private exchanges as Gwendolyn most properly divided her attention between him and Freddie on her left. Since this was an informal luncheon, she also addressed an occasional remark to Deborah, seated across the table.

But Miss Stormont had quite other concerns than Lord Crichton's courtship. Along the table, Perry had been placed beside Julie de Keroualle. He had put down his knife and fork and was now staring raptly at her, his mouth half-open and his eyes glazed.

There was a strange sinking feeling in Debs's stomach as she watched him. On her other side, Edouard was responding to his sister's teasing. Deborah caught the word *rôdeur*.

"Ah," she said turning to the *vicomte*, "do you have a prowler, too?"

"Too!" Julie clapped her hands and switched easily to English. "Do you mean, Mademoiselle Stormont, that you have also strangers up at the Bois?"

"I haven't seen them," Deborah admitted, "I've only heard of them. The butler saw them."

"Then he will know if it's Gonidec," Julie declared.

"Gonidec?" Deborah looked at the *vicomte*. He was a handsome young man, she realized, especially when he stopped scowling.

"Yes." Edouard nodded. "He was a footman here before the Revolution and he came to England with us."

"Yes, he was with us in Oxford." Julie nodded so vigorously that her dark curls bobbed. "Although I do not remember him myself, for I was too small. But, *figurez-vous*, Maman had to let him go. One day she found him in her room, actually going through her papers!"

"Indeed?" Lord Crichton joined the conversation. "And had you seen him since he was dismissed?"

"Not till last week. Then I saw a man I did not know in the pine wood. Later Edouard recognized him lurking round the gardens here."

"*Eh bien,* Julie, I do not know if one should say 'lurking.'" Her brother shrugged. "Gonidec was born in Beganne St. Pierre, after all. He may just want to visit his old home. It is harvest time, you know. Perhaps he is working here."

"Perhaps he's interested in treasure-hunting." Perry spoke breathlessly, his eyes still on Julie's face.

"*Oh là,*" she exclaimed, laughing. "Did you not hear, Monsieur Stormont, that he was with us in England? He must have known that Maman knew nothing of this lost treasure, that it was all a *blague.*"

After lunch the party went out into the gardens. Deborah thought Lord Crichton would now have his chance with Miss Phipps-Hedder. But to her surprise she felt Gwendolyn take her own arm.

"Will you let me show you over the grounds, Miss Stormont?"

"Thank you." Deborah did not look at Lord Crichton. "But please call me Deborah."

"And you must call me Gwendolyn." Miss Phipps-Hedder glanced round. The younger men were gathered about an ancient fowling piece that Edouard had brought to show them. Louise and the *vicomtesse* were enjoying a comfortable cose, their chairs drawn well back out of the afternoon sun. Julie and Lord Crichton were standing together on the steps down to the lawn, while they discussed the layout of the grounds.

If Beron were her fiancé, Deborah thought, she would not leave him alone in such fascinating company. But Gwendolyn appeared perfectly unperturbed as she tucked her arm more firmly into Deborah's and led her off.

"Now, this," she said, "is what they call the Allée des Chênes."

"It is quite lovely." Deborah looked admiringly at the two lines of tall trees whose branches met overhead to create a shadowy, leafy corridor.

"It's one of my favourite places in the château. It leads up to the most delightful grotto. There is the prettiest little fountain there, but Edouard says it was once an altar, where they sacrificed to the spirit of the wood. But I expect that he is only funning me, don't you think? For if such a thing ever happened, it must have been hundreds of years ago because, of course, I don't for a moment..."

Miss Phipps-Hedder, Deborah realized, was a prattle-box. The stream of gentle inanities ran on, needing only to be fuelled by an occasional "indeed" or "I quite agree."

By the time they had reached the grotto, Gwendolyn had exhausted the subject of the Allée and switched to Lord Crichton.

"I vow, Deborah, that I was never more surprised in my life when I turned and saw him standing there!" She sank down on one of the stone benches surrounding the little mermaid fountain. "I couldn't believe I was not dreaming for I had no notion, not even my papa had any notion, that he meant to come into France at all. Indeed, for one dreadful moment—" Gwendolyn shuddered dramatically "—I thought that perhaps Papa had sent him after me. But I was simply being goosish, for it was all the merest coincidence."

"But a happy one?" Deborah suggested as Gwendolyn paused at last for breath. "I collect that Lord Crichton was on his way to visit you when he was—" Deborah gulped "—when he was called away."

Miss Phipps-Hedder had pulled a fern leaf from those growing beside the bench. She twisted it in her finger, then tossed it to one side. "Yes," she said rather heavily and was silent for a moment. Then she rose. "Shall we go back now, Deborah? The gardens are much larger than this, of course, but not, Edouard says, nearly as large as some of the châteaux in the Loire. There, he says he has seen the most..."

Gwendolyn's conversation flowed over them as they came out of the Allée, to find the *vicomte* hovering there.

"Really, Gwendolyn," he scolded, "it is so chilly out of the sun. You should not go into the Allée without a wrap. You must recollect that you had that shock yesterday."

"But no, Edouard." Gwendolyn clasped his arm. "I never catch cold at this time of the year. It is quite remarkable, for in the Spring I am a positive martyr to the grippe, but once May is out I am invariably in high health.

Even Mama has said that it is truly astounding. It is just like the old English proverb—'n'er cast a clout till May is out,' you know—and I must tell you, Edouard . . .''

As she followed them up to the house, Miss Stormont sighed.

CHAPTER TWELVE

PEREGRINE, FREDDIE and Tante Louise were already at breakfast when Deborah came downstairs next morning.

"By George, Debs!" Perry exclaimed as he rose. "You do look well this morning. That pinky colour suits you."

Deborah's eyes met her aunt's. "Thank you, Perry," she said, demurely smoothing the silk that had once lined an opera cape for Madame d'Auray.

"In fact—" Perry peered closely at her "—you've been looking better all round since we came into France. Julie said yesterday that she thought you were beautiful. Dashed if I don't think she was right."

"Of course she was." Freddie looked reprovingly at his friend. "Anyone can see that Miss Stormont is a diamond of the first water."

"Freddie," said Deborah, much moved, "I thank you, but that is surely a rapper."

"Certainly not! I wouldn't flummery you, Deborah."

Seeing that Deborah was disconcerted by the turn in the conversation, Louise spoke to Peregrine. "You seemed to have much to say to Miss de Keroualle, Perry." She picked up her inevitable crochet. "She is a delightful girl, is she not?"

Perry flushed scarlet and his sister put down her roll and stared at him. "Oh, yes!" he said ardently. "She is a diamond, isn't she? I mean when she said that about you, Debs, I said I hadn't really noticed what you were wearing and do you know what she said?" He looked enquiringly at them. "It was the cleverest, most philosophical thing. I'll wager a monkey you'll never guess."

Mutely, his audience shook their heads.

"She said she was talking about inner beauty, the sort clothes had nothing to do with." He gazed triumphantly round the table. "Did you ever hear anything like that?"

"Most...most penetrating of her," Madame d'Auray murmured in carefully controlled tones. "Do you not agree, Freddie?"

Freddie had been gaping open-mouthed at his friend. He appeared to be waiting for Perry's remarks to reach a conclusion. However, at Louise's question, he shut his mouth, took a deep breath and said hurriedly, "Absolutely old chap, absolutely. Never heard the like, ever."

As to Deborah, she found herself unable to say anything at all. She could not take her eyes off Perry's face—that extraordinary mixture of pride and embarrassment. About her, the breakfast continued.

Lord Crichton arrived just as Louise was bidding them good-morning, as she set off about domestic affairs. Freddie and Perry also took their leave, this time to shoot pigeons in the countess's woods. Deborah said mechanical goodbyes and only after a long pause did she become aware that Beron had spoken to her.

"I beg pardon, my lord," she said, flushing, "I'm afraid I was wool-gathering. You were saying..."

"I asked if you would care to take your coffee on the terrace, Miss Stormont. It is another pleasant morning." As usual, Beron's voice was calm and even, though his grey eyes were very thoughtful as they studied her.

"Certainly." Deborah rose and carried her coffee out through the glass doors.

They sat at the round willow table and looked out over the lower terrace, the fountain and the surrounding fields. The only sound was the plash of the fountain and the twittering of swallows as they circled the honey-coloured barns.

"You seem somewhat *distraite* this morning, Miss Stormont." Beron's tone did not change but, somehow, Deborah felt he would not be easily fobbed off.

"Pray disregard my distraction, Lord Crichton. It is nothing at all."

"Now, Miss Stormont, you must have become weak-minded indeed, if you permit yourself to be overset by nothing." There was a smile in his lordship's voice and his manner was gently teasing.

Reluctantly she laughed. "But if I tell you, sir, you will simply rake me down again for my odiously managing ways!"

"*Touché,* Miss Stormont." His smile became a little wry. "But will you not give me another chance and let me try to redeem myself?"

"The thing is," Deborah said honestly, "that I fear you may well be right."

"My dear Miss Stormont!" Beron sounded shocked. "Can you have really said that! I am sure you are not at all well. Something monstrous must have happened. I beg you to confide in me instantly."

"Only if you call falling in love monstrous."

There was a silence. Then his lordship said in the ironic drawl she so disliked, "Am I to understand that you have fallen victim to Dr. Trewin's scholarly charms?"

"Really, my lord! How can you be so absurd? I wish you would be serious."

There was an upward curl at one corner of Beron's mouth. "I thought I was being so," he murmured. "I was

evidently fair and far out. If it is not you who is enamoured, who may it be?''

"Peregrine, of course!"

"Peregrine?" Lord Crichton's eyebrows rose. Then he
laughed. "Ah, I see—the entrancing Miss de Keroualle.''

"If you could have heard him before you came in this
morning! I should never have believed it if I hadn't been
there myself. And his face!''

"A little like a sheep with severe indigestion?''

"I suppose so." Her smile was fleeting.

"Then it is undoubtedly love," pronounced Beron, but
when Deborah did not respond, he concentrated for a
moment on stirring his coffee. Then he laid down his
spoon. "But surely," he said quietly, "this cannot be an
entirely unexpected event?''

"I . . . I do not understand you, my lord.''

"Peregrine is a personable young man. And—" he
paused and then went coolly on "—forgive me if I have
misjudged you, Miss Stormont, but I had not thought you
wished to keep him in leading strings.''

"Of course I don't!''

"Then surely it was inevitable that his fancy would be
caught by some female, sooner or later.'' He looked quizzically at her. "You might rather be grateful that his eye
has fallen on such a very unexceptionable object.''

Debs said nothing for a moment. She twisted her bowl
back and forth between her hands. "I suppose so," she
said unhappily. Then, with more heat, she burst out, "But
how could they possibly marry? Perry hasn't a groat and I
am very sure that the *vicomtesse* could not look with favour on such a connection.''

"You do not hunt, I believe, Miss Stormont?''

Deborah moved impatiently. "Of course I don't! What
can that signify?''

"There is a hunting maxim that you would do well to consider: don't rush your fences."

"Oh! You mean I may be leaping to—"

"Consider, Miss Stormont. Your brother met the lady only yesterday. He has spent what—three, maybe four hours—in her company, and that under the eye of her mother. And here you are, worrying about their marriage."

"It does sound ridiculous when you put it like that," Deborah owned, still fiddling with her coffee bowl.

Lord Crichton watched her under his lowered lids. Then he said very gently, "But there is more to it, isn't there?" When Deborah did not speak, he went on, "I do not wish to be impertinent, Miss Stormont, but I think Perry's infatuation has forced you to contemplate a rather unpalatable prospect."

"I think you must be a mind-reader, Lord Crichton." Her voice was very low.

"Hardly that. But I see you are troubled and I think perhaps you had not before really faced the fact that one day Perry must indeed marry and—" he added deliberately "—leave you."

"I wonder, my lord, if your friends appreciate your plain-speaking?" Deborah pushed a curl back behind her ear and tried to smile.

"Not all of them," Beron acknowledged. "I shouldn't, of course, say such things to you, if I did not think you perfectly capable of accepting the truth of them."

Deborah blinked. "I think you overestimate me, my lord."

"I doubt it," Beron said calmly. "But I do think you are anticipating. It is true that some people do form a lasting passion at that age, but it is equally true that one's first love is rarely one's last love."

"Was yours?" Deborah asked, greatly daring.

"Certainly not." Lord Crichton pretended to frown at her. Then he smiled reminiscently. "My first love was the landlady of the local tavern—an extremely, er, buxom lady, if I recall correctly."

"Your parents must have been horrified."

"Especially since the lady was already married. But," Beron continued with a chuckle, "it didn't matter to me because I never actually found enough courage to speak to her."

Deborah laughed and he stood and held out his hand to her. "Come, Miss Stormont, the good doctor tells me my leg requires exercise. So let us take a turn about the *étang.*"

They manoeuvred down the steps. As they passed the fountain, someone hailed them. It was Simon Trewin.

"May I join you, Miss Stormont and my lord?"

"Of course, Dr. Trewin." Debs nodded in a friendly way and Lord Crichton bowed. "I am glad to see you recovered."

"Of course, Miss Stormont. I pray you not to mention it further. It was an unfortunate accident."

"The Duchesse is a most unpredictable animal," his lordship murmured.

Simon Trewin ignored him. "I had some business this way later in the afternoon," he said to Deborah, "so I ventured to call again. Naturally I do not suppose you to have made up your mind yet, but I thought you might perhaps care for some more information. If it will not unduly bore his lordship, I shall explain my project more fully."

"Please feel free to make your representation, Dr. Trewin." Beron motioned to Debs and Simon to precede him on the path. He himself ambled on along behind them.

"As you may be aware, Miss Stormont," Trewin began, "there is increasing interest in the natural world. Many persons have taken to the woods and fields, collecting specimens, preserving them in flower-presses and the like. For many such enthusiasts an authoritative compendium would be highly desirable. I intend a fully coloured illustrated guide to the common flora of our island."

"I see that such a publication would surely be useful, Dr. Trewin. Indeed, I have often wished for such a volume myself. But tell me, sir, do you intend to include the fescues and other like plants?"

"What is your feeling on this matter, Miss Stormont?"

"Well, strictly speaking of course, they are grasses rather than flowers...."

"Just so. I think we might keep this first volume just for the flowers, then. We may well be thinking of other—" he spread his hands expansively "—more specialized editions."

"It sounds a massive project," Deborah said, "and I am aware, though doubtless you will be more familiar with such matters than I, that there have been many new discoveries in recent years. I recall reading that a Greater Butterwort, for instance had been found in Ireland. That is, I collect," she added, looking enquiringly at him, "the first time the plant has been documented in our islands?"

Trewin looked admiringly back at her. "I see I have chosen my colleague well, Miss Stormont."

She flushed a little at the warmth of his regard. "I'm highly flattered that you should have decided upon me as the illustrator."

"As soon as I saw your sketches I knew I could do with no one else. Tell me, does such talent run in your family?"

"I scarcely think so. My mother worked a little in wa-ter-colour, but I do not think them in any way remark-able."

"And your aunt, is she so inclined?"

"Tante Louise?" Debs smiled affectionately. "No, I think her artistic abilities lie in her crochet and in her lace-making."

"She is a widow, is she not?"

"Yes, my uncle was killed in the Terror."

"A sad time, Miss Stormont, but what a blessing that your aunt was able to salvage so much."

Deborah glanced behind her. She had thought she heard Lord Crichton speak, but his lordship was staring pen-sively into the long grass beside the path.

"Not really." She turned back to Simon. "It is thought that my uncle did try to make some provision against an uprising, but the speed of events overtook him."

"You spoke of treasure-hunters yesterday, Miss Stor-mont. I have heard tales of families who managed to se-crete their valuables and to retrieve them at a more favourable time. It occurred to me that such a tale could well encourage treasure-hunters."

"It all sounds rather romantical to me," Debs replied with some reserve. Charming as Dr. Trewin might be, she had no intention of discussing private family matters with him.

"Other families, I understand, were able to send word of such a cache to friends or relatives in England and in this way they were able to preserve at least some of their fortune. Your uncle was ideally placed to avail himself of such a scheme."

"One might think so, but as I said, events proved too swift for him." Deborah did not wish to pursue the sub-ject. Noting her reluctance, Trewin switched to a more humorous vein. "What, Miss Stormont? No secret passages? No mysterious documents? No half-burned treasure maps?"

"I think you must have been listening to village gossip." Deborah chuckled. "But here we are at the *étang*. Turning round to Lord Crichton again, she thought she caught movement out of the corner of her eye, but his lordship was contemplating the view, leaning on a staff he had picked up en route.

"How do you go on, my lord?" she asked. "Do you care to rest?"

"No, no, Miss Stormont. Pray continue your interesting discussion with Dr. Trewin."

"I must not monopolize Miss Stormont further," said Simon easily. "Many of the details will have to be discussed with the publisher, in any case."

"And that will be when you return to Oxford, after the Long Vacation?" asked Beron.

"As you say, my lord."

"Must be rather annoying for you to have been obliged to travel at such a time," Beron said sympathetically. "I know several Oxford fellows, and they are usually most anxious to use the Long Vacation to further their research projects."

Trewin had picked up a small stone. He threw it so that it skipped across the surface of the *étang*. "You have friends at Oxford, Lord Crichton? Perhaps we have acquaintances in common, then."

"I hardly think so," Lord Crichton murmured. "But you must be most anxious to return to your college, Trewin, and begin this most significant project."

"I am indeed. But as I told Miss Stormont, I have begun a study of French ferns, which I am reluctant to abandon."

"Ferns," Beron repeated, "not moulds?"

Deborah gave him a minatory glare. "Is there much difference between the English and French varieties, sir?"

"Oh, rather technical differences, Miss Stormont. I shall not bore you with them."

Debs turned her head again. She was sure she'd seen something moving at the corner of her eye. But the surroundings looked perfectly tranquil.

Lord Crichton gestured. "There must be much here to interest you, Trewin, in the way plants have naturalized themselves in an essentially artificial environment."

"Fascinating!" Trewin nodded vigorously. "Absolutely fascinating."

"Over here now," Deborah said, pointing to the hogweed, "is something I consider fascinating. Have you ever seen anything like this, Dr. Trewin?"

"Ah! I see what you mean, Miss Stormont." He walked over to study the plant more closely. He bent down to peer into the heart of the clump.

Deborah glimpsed a white flash speeding past. Trewin gave a sudden yelp as the Duchesse butted him into the very centre of the hogweed clump.

"Dr. Trewin!" Deborah was aghast.

His lordship bent down and, apparently absently, scratched the goat's head. The Duchesse stood, sniffing disparagingly, as though troubled by a bad smell.

"Trewin certainly believes in becoming involved with his work," he commented. "Though those thorns must be rather more uncomfortable than the moulds."

"Stop babbling and get me out of here!" Trewin shouted, wriggling frantically as he tried to free himself from the prickly stalks.

"Oh, for heaven's sake!" Deborah ran forward and tried to grasp Simon's hand.

Lord Crichton followed in a more leisurely fashion. "Now, Trewin," he said in his calm way, "take our hands and stop thrashing about like that or you'll have both Miss Stormont and me in on top of you. And besides, your coat will be in ribbons."

Both Debs and Beron hauled, and with a last effort they tugged Simon Trewin to his feet.

"That bloody animal!" He turned on the goat. "It's trying to kill me! This is the second time it's tried to murder me. It should be shot! It should be—" He advanced on the Duchesse with a decidedly murderous expression on his own face.

Hastily, Deborah gripped his arm. "Dr. Trewin," she said, attempting to soothe him. "I see you have some scratches on the back of your hands. Will you not come back to the house so they may be treated?"

Trewin put her aside. "I'm not going back to that madhouse," he said angrily. "There's probably a lunatic cat ready to spring on me or a deranged dog lurking round the corner. I'll say good day to you, Miss Stormont, and—" he glared inimically at the hogweed "—to your precious plant." He jerked out a bow, then strode off.

"Oh, dear." Deborah stared at his receding form. "Perhaps I should go after him."

"Not at all, Miss Stormont," Lord Crichton said. "He needs time to cool down, to reflect and besides—" he leant heavily on his stick "—I need your help."

Deborah looked suspiciously at him. "You?"

"My leg," Beron said, with an air of suffering bravely borne. "I fear I may have overtaxed it. I must ask for your arm on the way back."

Debs looked even harder at him. It was too fanciful, she told herself, to think that Beron was in some way responsible for the goat's actions. But he had definitely not condemned them. And now, look at him! He was feeding the Duchesse a handful of purple clover.

She could not feel that Lord Crichton liked Simon Trewin. But there was nothing she could put her finger on. It was just something in his tone, in his look....

But his lordship was gazing rather pathetically at her, his stick prominently displayed. She did not trust that expression, but she had no choice. With a sigh she moved to Lord Crichton's side.

Arm-in-arm, they made their way back to the house. And Deborah was so busy trying to define exactly what Beron's attitude to Simon Trewin was that she quite overlooked just how pleasant she found this manner of walking.

CHAPTER THIRTEEN

NEXT MORNING, Lord Crichton arose and took an early, solitary breakfast. He wandered down to the stables where he eyed the two riding horses kept by Madame D'Auray. He shrugged, thinking longingly of his own big grey, now rescued from the blacksmith and at his home in Surrey.

He decided he would walk a little. If he turned to the east, he could circle back through the pine wood and along the *étang*. It was a glorious, early-autumn morning. There was only the faintest tinge of yellow in the leaves to hint that winter was coming. Moodily, Lord Crichton broke off a branch and swished it idly as he walked. His leg, it appeared, had fully recovered from the weakness of yesterday.

The beauty of the morning did not raise his spirits. Though, he considered ruefully, it would be difficult to assign a precise cause to his discontent.

"What's the matter, my boy," he asked himself, "not getting cold feet, are you?"

Beron took a particularly vicious swipe at a fungus growing on a fallen log. He had to jump hurriedly backwards as it exploded in a shower of dry powder. He'd asked himself that same question on the Dover Road, he recalled.

And the answer was still the same: what was there to get cold feet about? Essentially the situation had not changed. True, his first meetings with Miss Phipps-Hedder had not gone entirely as planned, but some private conversation with her would easily remedy that.

Miss Phipps-Hedder was a sensitive girl, so his sudden appearance had naturally startled her. She simply needed to regain her equilibrium. Lord Crichton repeated this statement several times and at last succeeded in repressing a faint feeling of impatience at Gwendolyn's sensitivity.

He had not known that she was such a high-strung female. Nor, said another part of his mind, that she was such a rattle-pate. In fact, he must own that he knew very little of Gwendolyn.

He had met her at routs, balls, and Almack's. He had escorted her to two exhibitions at Burlington House and to a supper party at Vauxhall Gardens. But of course he had not been alone with her on any of these occasions. Lady Phipps-Hedder's notions were extremely nice, and much as she might welcome Beron's attentions, her chaperonage of her eldest daughter was strict and complete.

Once Beron had decided it was time to set up his nursery he had chosen Gwendolyn because she was well-bred, prettily mannered and possessed of a good deal of countenance. That he was always slightly bored in her company and had never discussed with her one issue of any importance to him had not struck him as significant obstacles. It was, after all, a wife he was seeking.

For which role, he reminded himself, Gwendolyn was eminently suited. The events of the past two weeks had in no wise altered that fact. If he hadn't had the misfortune to meet up with Deborah Stormont, he would have gone to Radwitch Hall and all would now be decently settled.

His lordship savagely beheaded a dandelion. None of these doubts would have entered his head if it hadn't been for that Stormont woman's interference!

And, he determined, no managing female was going to throw a rub in his way. By heaven, Lord Crichton vowed, he had set out to propose to Gwendolyn Phipps-Hedder, and whether in England or France, he was going to do just that!

Unaware that she was the subject of his lordship's mental defiance, Deborah was happily sketching at the *étang*. Her study of the hogweed was finished, but she had found another, rather intriguing specimen. It was a tall spike of purple flowers, a little like lavender, but thinner and a more intense purple. She had never seen the plant before and, as she drew, she thought she must ask Simon Trewin to identify it.

It was very tranquil here this morning. She could hear the rooks calling from the pines and every now and then a frog plopped into the lily-covered water. She was reminded of how Lord Crichton had lounged beside her.

It was odd, she thought, how relaxed they had been together. He had lowered that shield of irony and as for her—well, it was true her defences, too, had fal—

She looked up as she heard her name called. Gwendolyn Phipps-Hedder waved and hurried up to her.

"How are you, Deborah? Isn't it a lovely morning? Edouard—" she gestured to the *vicomte*, who was following behind "—wanted to show me this pond. It's got a special name but I forget what it is—"

Deborah opened her mouth to supply the word, but Miss Phipps-Hedder's sweet, breathless voice flowed relentlessly on. "So clever of the monks to think of it. And imagine what a relief it must have been to the villagers to have fresh fish to eat. However, I do declare that I can't care for trout myself, though the *vicomtesse*'s cook serves it in a most unusual sauce with, I collect, cream and cher-

vil and I must own that if anything could make me
like—''

"Bonjour, mademoiselle." Apparently deciding it was
useless to wait for a break in Gwendolyn's conversation,
the *vicomte* simply spoke through it, bowing to Deborah.

He looked very much happier this morning, she thought
as she responded. And what an attractive girl Gwendolyn
was, particularly with that light flush on her cheeks and
those brown eyes sparkling.

She leaned over to Debs and whispered mischievously.
"Just think, Deborah, here I am with Edouard, com-
pletely without a chaperon. Only consider what Mama
would say!" Safe in the knowledge that Lady Phipps-
Hedder was securely on the other side of the English
Channel, her daughter laughed delightedly.

"We are not exactly alone," the *vicomte* said. "My sister and—" he nodded to Debs "—your brother, *mademoiselle,* are regarding the menhirs."

Deborah put down her pencil. She had no idea that
Perry had gone over to the château that morning.

"But I find all those big old stones so, well, sinister."
Gwendolyn shuddered. "I didn't want to stay there at all.
It is much prettier here. In fact," she added with a luxu-
rious sigh, "I do adore Brittany, do you not, Deborah?"

This time Miss Stormont did not even attempt to answer, which was just as well, for Gwendolyn did not wait.
"It is not only the flowers, and the scenery and the people
who are so friendly, but this whole idea of buried treasure. Why, it's just like a lending library romance, is it
not?"

Deborah had little experience of such volumes, but she
nodded smilingly at Gwendolyn's enthusiasm.

The *vicomte,* however, was less amused. "If this were
such a romance, Gwendolyn," he said with a snort, "then

there would be such a treasure and we should find it and—'' his young face was suddenly bleak ''—we should all live happily ever after. Unfortunately,'' he continued, and his voice was bitter, ''none of these things is true.''

Gwendolyn's brown eyes filled with tears. She laid her hand on his arm. ''Oh, Edouard,'' she said softly, ''you promised you would not think of these things.''

For a moment, they looked in each other's eyes. Then the *vicomte* laughed shortly, patted Gwendolyn's hand and gently disengaged it. ''I think we should rejoin Julie and Perry,'' he said. ''Your brother is joining us for lunch, Miss Stormont. Will you honour us also?''

''Thank you.'' Deborah felt all her apprehensions flooding back. Two days ago, they'd almost had to drag Perry to the château; now he seemed set to spend the whole day there. ''But I think both of us cannot abandon my aunt.''

''And, Deborah,'' Gwendolyn said, ''there is such exciting news! The *vicomtesse* has decided to let us have a ball. We shall send you a card, of course, once we have decided exactly when it is to be. She thinks that with you here, and some other residents and visitors, that there are sufficient people to make it a success. Is that not delicious news! I have the most charming dress and I shall—''

''It's not exactly a ball.'' Edouard cut in in his usual way, and as was apparently also usual, Gwendolyn accepted his interruption with unimpaired good humour. ''It will be like a supper dance. Nothing like the grand affairs you have been used to in London, Miss Stormont.''

Debs was still chuckling over this remark when they had said goodbye. She watched the two make their way round the pool, Edouard's hand protectively cupping Gwendolyn's elbow. As she watched, a slight frown grew between her dark brows.

What was it Lord Crichton had said? *Don't rush your fences.* And, unless she was greatly mistaken, this was not her affair at all. She must not speculate any further.

She picked up her sketch-book, but she did not reach for her pencil. Instead she sat idly flipping through the pages.

"Lost in thought, Miss Stormont?" Simon Trewin came up the path from the Bois.

Deborah laughed a little self-consciously. "Good morning, Dr. Trewin. Are you feeling better now?" Instinctively, she looked around. But she could see no lurking white shape.

"It was nothing, Miss Stormont." He, too, looked rather warily around the *étang*. "I came to apologize for my bad temper yesterday. I am afraid I was quite rude to you." He looked ruefully towards the hogweed.

"Pray don't regard it," Deborah told him. "I am quite out of patience with the Duchesse and no one could wonder at your being put quite out of frame yourself."

"You are too kind, Miss Stormont." He looked down at her pencil and paper. "Now, which of these specimens has attracted your attention this morning?"

"I was intrigued by this plant here." She indicated the purple spear. "Can you tell me its name, Dr. Trewin?"

He bent to examine it, turning it from side to side, frowning as he ran his hand over the leaves. Then he slowly shook his head. "It may be a Continental variety of purple loosestrife, but there are certain differences, in the leaf structure, for instance." He straightened up with a self-deprecating smile. "Have I disgraced myself utterly in your eyes, Miss Stormont? I assure you I am not nearly so ignorant of British flora."

"You are funning, Dr. Trewin. Naturally I understand that you cannot be an expert in everything."

"You are very kind, Miss Stormont, and—" he glanced at her sketch-book "—very talented."

Debs looked away and he went on. "Have you made many such sketches since your arrival in France?"

Deborah nodded. "A few. Here is one of the geraniums in the front urns and here is a study of some hydrangeas in the garden. This, of course, is the menhir field." She paused for a moment. "Look at this group of the more upright stones. They look rather like hands reaching up out of the ground, don't they? And here is the hogweed, of course, and over here—" She stopped and looked at Simon Trewin.

The scholar had made a sudden, sharp gesture. "Sorry, Miss Stormont. A spider fell on my sleeve. I'm afraid I rather dislike them."

Deborah smiled. "Many people do. It is fortunate, then, that you did not go into entomological studies."

"Indeed." He laughed. "And I am grateful for other reasons, too." His gaze rested warmly on her. "For if I had not become interested in botany, I should not have met you, Miss Stormont."

Deborah shifted uneasily and kept her eyes on her sketch-book. She knew she should make some graceful response but she could think of nothing to say.

"Forgive me," Simon Trewin said quietly, "I had no wish to distress you."

Deborah regained control of herself and replied as coolly as she could, "Not at all, Dr. Trewin. Did you wish to speak further of your compendium?"

"I wish I had time, Miss Stormont. But I have an appointment. A farmer back there—" he jerked his head "—has some problems with blight and I promised I'd have a look. But I felt I must come to apologize. Your aunt told me you were sketching back here, so I ventured to disturb you and," he added casually as he picked up the sketchbook and flipped through it, "of course to enjoy another look at your work."

"You flatter me, sir."

"I don't, you know, Miss Stormont. If the book should be a success, it will be largely due to your work." He bowed and took his leave, promising to call again soon.

For a stranger to the neighbourhood, Deborah reflected, he certainly seemed to find lots to do. But it was praiseworthy of him to put his expertise at the disposal of the local farmers.

She took up her pencil again, but her enthusiasm for further drawing had evaporated. She packed up her satchel and glanced at her watch-brooch. She still had some time before lunch. She would take a walk, perhaps over to the menhirs.

Still thinking of Simon Trewin, she set off through the woods. He had been most kind in his remarks on her work. But some of his comments had had a more personal tone....

In Salisbury, Deborah had known few eligible young men. One or two friends of Perry's had developed tendres for her. But she had easily dealt with them, and her own heart had remained untouched.

But Simon Trewin was older and more sophisticated than any of these boyish admirers. Deborah regretted her inexperience. Was it possible that he was actually, well, fixing an interest in her?

Or was she reading too much into polite conversation? That, she told herself, might well be true. For, though she must blush to own it, there had been times when she thought Lord Crichton, too, was actually... but that was too far-fetched. She did not understand the ways of the world.

No, what she might do was speak to Tante Louise, provided, of course, that it did not make her look too odiously conceited. . . .

She blinked a little as she came out from the wood into the bright sunlight. She moved forward to stand beneath the pine till her eyes adjusted. There was a rustle in the pine needles to one side. As Deborah turned her head, there was a crushing blow and a burst of blinding light.

She had just time to think that the pine boughs must be lower than she had remembered, before she fell into the darkness and silence.

CHAPTER FOURTEEN

SHE WAS BACK on the *Orient Wave,* Debs thought, and they must be in a storm, for they were pitching desperately about. She felt dizzy and clutched at what she thought were blankets.

"Be easy, Miss Stormont," soothed a soft, familiar voice.

Her eyes flew open. She was not at sea. She was—Deborah blushed scarlet—she was in Beron Crichton's arms, grasping his coat lapels.

She let go of them, as if they were on fire. "Put me down at once, sir," she demanded, mortified that her voice did not remain steady.

"I shall, of course, if you feel truly well." Beron looked down at her.

Those grey eyes and that long mobile mouth were so disturbingly close that Deborah turned her head and tried to lean a little further back, out of his arms.

Lord Crichton did not attempt to suppress his chuckle. "If you lean over like that, Miss Stormont, you will unbalance both of us and we will end up on the ground. And that, let me assure you, would be a far more compromising position."

Angrily, Deborah snapped her head back to retort. She opened her mouth, but a wave of nausea overwhelmed her and she fell back against his chest.

Lord Crichton's grip tightened. When she could speak Debs said faintly, "What happened to me?"

She did not see Beron's eyebrows rise. "I hoped you could tell me, Miss Stormont. I was out walking and when I came to the menhir field, I found you lying beneath the pine tree. Did you perhaps come over faint?"

"N-n-n-o-o." Deborah rubbed her head. "I think I bumped my head. I was just looking at the stones, thinking about my sketch about how clear and straight the shadows were, how the menhirs really did look like fingers, reaching up out of the gr—" She sighed and put a hand to her throbbing temples. "I don't remember any more. I suppose I must have walked into an overhanging branch."

Lord Crichton didn't answer. Looking up at him from under her lashes, Debs saw that his lips had narrowed, but she could not read the expression in his eyes.

Feeling her gaze, he said easily, "Ah yes, that would account for it. But here we are at the Bois. Your aunt will see to you now."

Deborah was suddenly filled with embarrassment. She didn't want anyone to see her like this. "I am most grateful to you, my lord," she said as formally as she could, "but I believe I may manage, if you will be so good as to put me down."

He paused at the top of the terrace steps. "You must be feeling better, Miss Stormont."

She looked warily at him as he set her carefully on her feet.

"You have," he remarked, smiling at her, "resumed your governessy air. That must mean you feel the situation slipping out of your control and are well enough to want it back."

Deborah took a deep breath. "Lord Crichton..." she began awfully. But she had overestimated her recovery. Her knees seemed to fold beneath her and she would have fallen if Beron had not caught her.

"Deborah! My lord!" Tante Louise had come out onto the terrace. She stared at her niece, sagging against Lord Crichton.

Belatedly, Deborah realized what a figure she must cut. She could feel her hair loose about her face. There were grass stains on her skirts and she could see pine needles stuck in her spencer.

"Miss Stormont met with an accident in the wood," Beron explained, careful not to remove his arms from about Deborah. "I was about to carry her inside but she, ah, preferred to walk."

"Really, Debs." Madame d'Auray looked anxiously at her niece's white face. "This is no time to be missish. Pray follow me, my lord. We must get her to bed immediately."

With a bow, Beron bent and effortlessly lifted Deborah. "Now, Miss Stormont," he said, "suppress your natural, maidenly modesty and put at least one arm about my neck. The stairs at the Bois are steep and I have no desire to add to your injuries by dropping you down them." He smiled at her mulish expression. "Tomorrow you may ring a peal over me for my odiously encroaching ways."

"But for today, it seems I have no choice." Gingerly, Deborah slid an arm along his broad shoulders.

"None at all," agreed Beron cheerfully as he set off after his hostess.

As they hurried upstairs, Beron explained what had happened to Madam d'Auray.

"The menhir field!" she exclaimed. "Surely she did not run into any of these prowlers."

"Prowlers?" Beron checked for a moment. "You have been troubled by prowlers again?"

"Not exactly troubled. Two men have been seen by the servants. We just assumed they were these tiresome treasure-hunters. But such persons have never resorted to violence."

"Miss Stormont is of the opinion she struck her head on a low-hanging branch."

"That sounds rather more likely. In here, my lord. Pray place her directly on the bed." Louise pulled the bell for Marie-Claire. "Would you add to your goodness, my lord, and tell Bigard to send for the doctor, please?"

"I don't need a doctor," Deborah protested, though she was glad to find herself in bed. "I just banged—" She moaned as she lifted her head rather too quickly.

Marie-Claire appeared at the door. She gasped at the sight of her mistress and Madame d'Auray hastened over to give her instructions.

Lord Crichton stood down one step on the bed-stairs and stopped to look at Deborah, his face on a level with hers. "Poor Miss Stormont," he said gravely. "I'm afraid you must consent to being managed for a while." Gently, he touched her hand, lying white and still on the feather quilt. He stood looking down at her for a moment and then took his leave to go in search of Bigard and Peregrine.

After speaking to the butler, he found that young gentleman moodily tossing pebbles into the fountain.

"Bigard thought," he said casually, "that you had gone over to the château."

"Had lunch there," said Perry gloomily. "But the *vicomtesse* took Julie and Gwendolyn off to visit some dreary old person in Redon." He tossed his last pebble and thrust his hands into his pockets. "I can't think why she should go bothering the old lady like that. People with the grippe need quiet, not hordes of people trailing all over their house."

"Shockingly inconsiderate," agreed his lordship, shaking his head. "But tell me, Perry—" he slipped his arm into the younger man's, drawing him on to stroll "—what exactly is all this about treasure-hunters? I have heard remarks about a buried treasure, but I think it's time I got it clear."

"Only a hum, if you ask me." Perry was not to be easily diverted. "I searched the whole house myself, and there's not a secret panel or hidden room in it or I'm a Dutchman."

"But tell me just how the tale originated," Beron urged. "With your late uncle, was it not?"

Perry shrugged, but contrived to give a more or less coherent account, even providing an accurate, if execrably accented, rendition of the rhyme.

"But," he concluded, "I don't believe that's really got anything to do with the treasure at all. I'll wager it's just one of those word games Uncle Raoul seems to have been nutty on."

They had mounted the steps and now turned the corner of the house. They found the Duchesse sunning herself on the front steps. Beron leaned down to scratch her ears.

"If it's a code," he said, "one ought to be able to make something of it. Say it to me again, Perry."

"Eh?" Perry sat down also, leaning his back against the Duchesse. She grunted aggrievedly, but did not move.

Beron had taken out a small leather bound book and a gold mechanical pencil. "Say the rhyme again," he repeated and wrote as Perry recited. He frowned at the paper.

"Well?" Perry demanded. "Can you make anything of it?"

"Not really," said Beron slowly, "and that, you know, is rather surprising."

Perry blinked. "Why?"

"Because, my dear boy, after I was invalided out, I spent some time in the Cipher Department."

"Spies!" Perry's eyes widened.

"Not perhaps as you imagine," said Beron, smiling. He stared at his book again and, taking advantage of his position, the Duchesse laid her head across his knees. "One can't always break a code, but one can usually see some sort of pattern in it. But I don't recognize any such thing here."

"What does it mean, then?"

"It may mean that this is no true code, but as you say, a kind of puzzle."

"Can we solve it?"

"I suspect that there is some play on words and their meanings involved." He muttered a few lines to himself. "Probably there is just one significant point here, and the rest is added as a filling, to try to distract the solver and make things more difficult. But without knowing, it is impossible to say what is important and what is mere padding."

"Then we shall never find out what it means?"

"One usually needs more information—something to suggest what was in the writer's mind." He frowned down at the paper and rather absently scratched the goat's ears. The gold eyes closed as the Duchesse slipped into a blissful trance.

"It might be a riddle or conundrum, maybe even a mnemonic, a device to jog the memory," Beron murmured.

"That, I suppose, makes it even harder to decipher?"

"Yes, I'm afraid so, Perry. We'd need to know a lot more about your uncle and what he may have been thinking at the time he wrote the rhyme."

"Thought it was too good to be true." Perry broke off a mauve geranium flower and began to shed the petals. "Mind you, a long-lost treasure is just what we need around here."

Lord Crichton studied him for a moment. Then, as gently as he could, he told Peregrine of Deborah's accident.

"But is she all right?" Perry leapt up, scattering mauve flowers.

"I believe so. The doctor has been summoned and your aunt and her maid are with her."

"I must go and see her right—"

"Later, I think, Perry. She will do better for some rest."

"But how could it happen? Debs ain't at all the sort of person to go bargin' into trees."

"There is some suggestion there may have been strangers poking about. Some of these treasure-hunters, I collect."

Perry's face darkened. "These—what do you call 'em, these *rôdeurs?* Do you mean one of these awful brutes might have attacked her?"

Beron looked rather inscrutably at him. "Perhaps she might have come upon them as they were engaged on some nefarious business in the menhir field over by the—"

"By heaven! I'll give 'em treasure! By the stones and the pine wood you say? I'll go over right now and if there are any of those villains lurking about, I'll rout 'em!"

Beron watched as Perry hurried off. He felt quite sure the pine wood and the menhir field were now innocent of strangers. But the search would vent Perry's feelings and occupy him for the moment.

But I wonder, he said to himself. He tapped his pencil lightly on his notebook and frowned at the page. *I very much wonder . . .*

The Duchesse made no response, except to blow her breath noisily through her nose. Beron stayed where he was, staring out over the lawns and bordering poplars of Le Bois qui Chante.

When he heard approaching footsteps, he turned his head. Simon Trewin was hastening towards him. He stopped when he saw the goat.

"Ah, Trewin," said Beron urbanely, snapping his notebook shut and returning it to his pocket. "Won't you join me?" He gestured to the steps. "You need not fear her grace. She is," he said, scratching the ducal ear, "quiescent at present."

Trewin eyed the goat darkly. He edged himself down on the top step, making sure his legs were as far away from the Duchesse as possible. "What is this I hear, Crichton?" he asked. "I have just met Bigard and the local doctor, hastening to see Miss Stormont. What has happened? Has she taken ill?"

"I regret to inform you that she has met with an unfortunate accident."

"An accident?" Trewin repeated blankly. "What sort of accident? Can she talk? Has she said what happened?"

"Miss Stormont is able to give no account of the event," said Beron slowly. "A loss of memory is not uncommon in such cases, as I understand. She recalls only that she went for a walk in the pine wood. I came upon her lying in a faint beneath a tree."

Trewin looked searchingly at him. "But young Peregrine pushed past me, muttering something about an attack by these treasure-hunters."

Lord Crichton smiled indulgently. "Ah, Perry is an impetuous young man. He believes in this buried-treasure nonsense and has become persuaded that his sister disturbed the hunters at some crucial stage." He laughed, as though amused by Perry's naiveté.

Trewin also smiled. "I suppose such a story is bound to catch the boy's imagination. But surely such persons would not normally resort to violence."

Beron shrugged. "I do not think we need pay much attention to Perry's overheated suspicions. Miss Stormont herself is of the opinion that her head struck a branch."

"Indeed? That is surely a more rational explanation than enraged treasure-hunters. Insofar," he added with a whimsical smile, "as this whole treasure business may be deemed rational at all."

"You are not a believer in this picturesque local legend, then, Trewin?" His lordship tugged gently at the Duchesse's long, silky ears.

"Who can say?" the other returned lightly. "I should suppose many families tried to secure something against the coming storm."

"Precious few of them succeeded," Beron said tartly. "I had not thought to find such a romantical streak in a scientist, Trewin."

The Duchesse opened her eyes and her amber glance fell on Trewin. Her nostrils flared and he hastily drew his legs farther up onto the terrace.

"You are probably right, my lord. But one cannot wonder at how seductive such a story must appear to those who have a fanciful streak."

"Yes." Crichton sighed. "It is a very rare person who realizes that things are not always what they seem."

The Duchesse raised her head from Beron's knee. She stared steadily at Trewin, lifting her upper lip and exposing her long sharp teeth. Her expression would have done justice to the Iron Duke, inspecting an untidy and insubordinate subaltern.

Trewin scrambled hastily to his feet and backed away. "I think I shall just go in and enquire how the doctor found Miss Stormont. Give you good afternoon, Crichton."

"Good afternoon," his lordship responded politely.

Snuffling ominously, the Duchesse watched until Trewin had turned the corner of the house. Then, with a sigh, she settled down again.

Rather absently, Beron resumed petting the goat, but his gaze wandered out to the lawns and the lengthening shadows of the poplars. Two vertical lines formed between his fine brows while his other hand beat a gentle tattoo on the pocket where he had stowed his notebook. His lips moved as he soundlessly repeated the words of the rhyme.

CHAPTER FIFTEEN

MUCH TO DEBORAH'S CHAGRIN, Tante Louise insisted that she spend the next day in bed.

"For, you know, the doctor said rest and quiet were what you needed."

"But I am not such a poor thing that I must cling to my bed," Deborah protested.

"That has nothing to do with it," Madame d'Auray declared firmly. "You are a sensible girl and you are going to behave in a sensible way."

Deborah pulled a face. "I am always being sensible."

Louise raised her eyebrows. "Would you prefer to be nonsensical?"

Reluctantly, Deborah laughed. "Perhaps just a trifle frivolous."

"Well." Her aunt fluffed up the pillows and slipped them back into place. "You will have your chance, for the *vicomtesse* has decided that Friday is the day of her ball. There you may frivol to your heart's content."

Deborah passed a hand over her head. "I seem to recollect Gwendolyn's saying something about it yesterday. Perry will be so pleased."

"And you?" Madame d'Auray sat down in a bedside chair and picked up her crochet.

"What do you mean, Tante?"

"You say Perry will be pleased, but what are your own feelings?"

"Why, I shall be pleased too but, Tante Louise, don't you think I'm a little . . . well . . . *old* for such things?"

Louise put down her hook. "Not in years," she said, giving her niece a very direct look.

"I—I don't understand."

"You have had too much responsibility, too soon, *ma chère,* but you are still a young girl you know and," she added gently, "you have not had a lot of opportunity to experience such things as balls, so you need not put on such matronly airs."

Deborah looked rueful. "Oh, dear, do I really sound matronly?"

"Fortunately, not too often. But don't do it at the ball. Otherwise—" Louise looked mischievous "—you may frighten off your suitors."

"I don't know what you can mean, Tante."

Madame d'Auray laughed. "Well now, Dr. Trewin was much concerned to hear of your accident and these—" she gestured to a large bowl of yellow chrysanthemums on the windowsill "—arrived most promptly this morning."

"I don't even know if Dr. Trewin has been invited to the dance."

"I should think so. After all, my dear, this area is not exactly overflowing with personable—and eligible—young men." Louise picked up the frothy length of lace and began to work again. "There is no doubt that Lord Crichton has been invited."

"Oh, yes?" Deborah tried to give a tone of polite interest to her voice.

Louise's black eyes were dancing but she kept them on her handiwork. "His lordship was also much concerned over your ill health."

"It must have been rather a shock for him to find me lying there." And, she added to herself, he must have been quite disgusted by the state of disarray she had presented. "But, you are mistaken, Tante Louise, Lord Crichton is only expressing the interest good manners demand."

"Do you think so?" Madame d'Auray slipped the hook through three stitches together, then wound the wool over it again, pulled it through and held up the work to contemplate the result.

"I do." Deborah was firm. "He is not at all interested in me. In fact, in confidence, Tante, I may tell you that Lord Crichton's interest has been fixed in Miss Phipps-Hedder."

"Indeed?" Louise wrapped the white thread about her finger again. "I did not observe any signs of intimacy between them."

"The engagement is not to be announced as yet, so any such intimations would not be proper."

"To my eyes," her aunt pursued, "the girl seemed more nervous than enamoured of Lord Crichton."

Deborah sat up straighter. "Oh, I don't think so, Tante Louise. He is much older than she, of course, so a little diffidence on her part is entirely natural."

"Perhaps so." Louise squinted at her work again. "But, do you know, Debs, men of that stamp are not often charmed by schoolroom chits, however pretty."

Deborah twisted a corner of the sheet. "But I collect it is all settled."

"Then there is nothing more to be said." Her aunt rolled up her work and replaced it in her workbag. "But now," she added as she stood up, "I think you need to get some rest." She stopped at the door and smiled back at her niece, who looked uncharacteristically tiny in the huge bed. "If you wish to be frivolous, then contemplate the coming ball. I have a little idea myself, and Marie-Claire and I shall contrive a gown as a surprise for you."

"Thank you, thank you, Tante Louise..." Deborah's eyes were closing. "Thank you."

AFTER A LONG NAP, Deborah felt a little cheerier, and she was just finishing a hearty lunch when Perry bounced in.

"How are you, old girl?" Perry kissed her cheek and dropped into the armchair. "Dashed if it don't seem odd to see you languishing in bed."

"Not for long, I hope," Debs said, laughing. "I'm just doing this to please Tante Louise."

"What happened anyway?" he asked. "How did you damage your head?"

"A goosish thing to do, I know. I went to look at the megaliths and I don't remember much else. I suppose I must have walked into one of the pine branches."

"I went back there when Beron told me what had happened. I thought perhaps one of these prowlers might have—"

"I didn't see anyone."

"Nor did I," said Peregrine regretfully. "But," he continued, cheering up, "I did find traces of 'em. Someone has been digging all around some of the stones."

"Whatever for?" Debs stared at him. "Those stones go deep into the ground. Why would anyone try to dig them up? If they wanted them for building, like the farmers at Avebury, all they had to do was use the ones that have fallen over."

Perry shrugged. "I'll wager there's some reason for it," he said darkly.

She looked rather anxiously at him. Apparently he was much as usual, but there was a worrying undertone, a new intensity in his manner.

"What are your plans today, Perry?"

He picked up the vinaigrette from the bedside table and fiddled with the tasselled silver case. "Freddie's coming over. He's heard some more about that English fellow who's nosing about. Apparently he's put up in an inn there. He's been asking a lot of questions, Freddie's aunt heard. Freddie thinks we may try to pick up his trail. And—" his voice was elaborately casual "—we may just drop in at the château, to thank the *vicomtesse* for her invitation, you know."

"You will enjoy the ball, won't you, Perry?"

Her brother got up and paced restlessly about the room. "Oh, yes, I shall enjoy it, Debs. After all, what else do I have to look forward to?" He looked at her with a new bitterness in his eyes.

"Oh, Perry." Deborah held out her hands and Perry pressed them.

"What a care-for-nought I am," he said remorsefully. "Prattling on like this and giving you the headache, if you don't already have it. I'd best be off." He kissed her again and took his leave with a cheery wave.

But Deborah was not deceived. Lord Crichton might talk of an infatuation, but she thought Perry's feelings ran deeper than that. If only there were some possibility of a happy ending, but try as she would, she could find no solution.

Nevertheless, Deborah's spirits rose as Friday approached. Indeed, an air of excitement seemed to pervade the entire house. A new evening suit was being sewn for Perry in the village. The whole procedure was overseen by Freddie, who insisted on daily fittings and alterations that both entertained and enraged the village seamstress.

Dr. Trewin called again to enquire after Miss Stormont and to leave a basket of late peaches. Lord Crichton, however, seemed least affected by anticipation of the ball.

Indeed, Deborah had scarcely seen him for two days. He was, she understood, spending a lot of time up at the château. And that, Miss Stormont told herself, was only to be expected of a man in his position. Perhaps an announcement might be made at the ball....

However, Lord Crichton's actions were hardly those of an ardent suitor. In truth, he spent more time with the *vicomtesse* than with Miss Phipps-Hedder. In these conversations, they seemed to dwell at length on the past.

Beron listened attentively to the *vicomtesse*'s reminiscences and seemed to find particular interest in her late husband's hobbies. The *vicomtesse* displayed several examples of the *vicomte*'s conundrums, puns and word games. Lord Crichton was gratifyingly impressed with these and even went so far as to request permission to copy several of them into his own notebook.

But he did not entirely forsake his duties as pretender to Miss Phipps-Hedder's hand. He escorted Gwendolyn on a trip to the village. This outing, it might be presumed, would have provided his lordship an admirable opportunity for broaching their joint future but, although he was very thoughtful, he made no attempt to speak of anything other than conventional matters.

Miss Phipps-Hedder noticed nothing of his abstraction. She had recovered from her initial nervousness of him and since he showed no signs of marrying her out of hand, she was now quite at ease in his company. She bubbled happily on, her thoughts and conversation centred on the ball and not at all on her supposed suitor's lack of enthusiasm.

There was, after all, Beron reflected, a kinship between Sir Rodney and his daughter: what Gwendolyn lacked in volume, she made up in quantity.

He marvelled particularly at her lung capacity. If she had paused for breath at all, then he had missed that brief respite. But he was perfectly *au fait* as to Gwendolyn's views on the wearing of mittens at lunch-time, on the Breton habit of drinking cider at all hours of the day, on the superiority of English gardens over French ones, on Gwendolyn's pleasure in the château and the changes she would like to see there, on the perfect amiability of the *vicomtesse,* on the details of the gown she would wear at the ball, and on, he thought wryly, at least twenty-five other matters in which he had not the least interest.

His admiration for Lady Phipps-Hedder grew. It was clearly only her mother's presence which had restrained Gwendolyn in London. However, he told himself, once they were married, she would have the household to organize.

With any luck, she would be too busy to pursue such trivia. And, of course, as a married couple, they would have their separate interests. In London, Gwendolyn would have her own friends with whom to discuss such concerns.

Rather disconcertingly, Lord Crichton realized he did not find these reflections entirely consoling. Perhaps, he thought, he might mention the whole matter to Miss Stormont. She was, after all, a sensible woman. One could talk to her and she did not rattle on about all sorts of fribbles and—

Here, my boy! Lord Crichton pulled himself up short. What was he thinking of? Let the Stormont female look after her own affairs. It was all her fault that he was in this bumblebroth as it is. But the intrusion of Miss Stormont into his thoughts led to another reflection: What would *she* wear to this ball? She certainly looked better since they'd come into France. It must have been the aunt's doing.

Thank heavens they'd never seen that puce garment again. But what would she choose for the ball? Yellow might look well with that colouring, a blue perhaps....

Now, his lordship had been bored to death at some of the most elaborate entertainments in some of the most splendid houses in London, so it was not to be expected that he would be much thrilled by the prospect of a modest supper dance in an obscure French village.

But, oddly, he found himself drawn into the expectation that pervaded the Bois. Madame d'Auray seemed constantly closeted with Marie-Claire, both of them examining swatches of fabric, tulle roses or lengths of ribbon.

Freddie, his lordship was convinced, travelled with suitable attire for every imaginable occasion. But Mr. Wimpole had thrown himself with enthusiasm into the task of readying Peregrine for the ball. Apart from relentlessly but politely harrying the seamstress, he had determined to teach Perry to tie a perfect Trône d'amour.

The two young gentlemen retired upstairs for hours at a time. From behind closed doors issued strange oaths and imprecations. Stone-faced, Walton ferried ever more supplies of starched rectangles upstairs.

His lordship decided that Miss Stormont was the only one to maintain her equilibrium. He said as much as he came across her reading in the upstairs sitting-room.

Smiling, Deborah laid aside her book. "Alas, you flatter me, my lord. I must own that I too am all a-twitter. But my aunt has undertaken to surprise me with a gown, so I have nothing to do but possess my soul in patience."

"Oh! So that accounts for the ribbons and silks I see her festooned in."

Deborah chuckled. "I keep encountering her and Marie-Claire and I have to turn my head and promise not to peek."

"A surprise, is it?" His lordship repeated the words thoughtfully, the ghost of an idea forming in his head. "I see. I must hope then that I do not discommode her too much, for I have remembered a matter upon which I must consult her."

Miss Stormont watched him leave. Then, with a little shrug, she picked up her book. Lord Crichton had obviously been repelled by her display of enthusiasm. She had none of the proper *ennui* expected of a lady of fashion and nothing she could do would persuade Beron Crichton that she was anything but a gauche provincial.

Meanwhile, his lordship went quickly downstairs and there at the door of the breakfast room was Madame d'Auray.

"No, Marie-Claire." She shook her white head. "I don't think we shall use the silver netting. I think we had best keep it very simple." She looked up and saw Beron. "Did you wish to speak with me, my lord?"

"Yes, *madame*. I have a proposal to lay before you."

Louise raised her eyebrows and gestured Beron into the room. As he unfolded his plan, the twinkle in her black eyes grew brighter.

When his lordship paused hopefully, she said, "Why no, my lord. I see nothing exceptionable in such an undertaking. I am sure we may rely on your discretion and good taste."

"Of course, of course." Beron rose, as though anxious to be on his way. "I suppose I shall have to go as far as Rennes?"

"Certainly you will find better gold and silversmiths there and your choice will be much improved. You may, of course, take a horse or carriage as you please."

"Thank you, *madame*. I had best leave at once, then."

"If you please, my lord," she said, touching his arm, "may I prevail upon you to drop a word in Perry's ear? He has not your experience in the world."

"Of course, but," Beron replied with a grin, "Freddie's notions are extremely nice. I expect he has been before me there."

"Or Dr. Trewin," said Louise blandly.

"Trewin?"

"Yes. He has already made a similar enquiry of me."

"Indeed." Lord Crichton's grey eyes met Madame d'Auray's black ones. "He is a fellow who likes to be prepared, is he not?"

Her gaze did not waver. "I think he is not the only one, my lord."

"I think not." Beron was pensive for a moment. "I collect that Miss Stormont is now completely recovered from her, er, accident?"

"Certainly, my lord. She has suffered no ill effects."

"Then, to keep her in this happy state, I beg you to ensure that she is not again found alone on the edge of the menhir or any other field."

Madame d'Auray's white brows rose. "Do you think it necessary, my lord?"

"I think," Lord Crichton said slowly and deliberately, "that it is better to be safe than sorry."

"In that case, my lord, I shall certainly follow your recommendation."

Lord Crichton took his leave, and Louise went back to consult Marie-Claire in an extremely thoughtful mood.

Deborah found it strange that Beron should suddenly discover pressing business in Rennes. She mentioned her feeling both to Louise and Perry, but they were too caught up in their own affairs to do more than mutter and rush off. However, when Simon Trewin called the next day, and heard of his lordship's departure, he looked quite startled.

"In Rennes?" he repeated, as they sat by the fountain. "Is this not rather sudden?"

Deborah was watching the swallows circle overhead. "I did not know he was planning to travel, but there is no reason why he shouldn't, I suppose."

Trewin frowned. "I understood you to be old friends."

"Our acquaintance with his lordship," said Deborah coldly, "is not of long standing nor, I assure you, sir, is it particularly intimate."

"I beg your pardon, Miss Stormont." Trewin seemed relieved by her declaration. "I may say then, without offending you, that I find much of Crichton's behaviour incomprehensible."

Privately Deborah agreed that his lordship's manner could be not only incomprehensible, but positively infuriating. Still, she would not commit the solecism of discussing him with Dr. Trewin.

"I believe, sir," she said somewhat repressively, "that you should discuss your puzzlement with Lord Crichton himself."

"Yes," Simon said, but Deborah thought his mind was not on her suggestion. "Peregrine tells me," he went on, "that Crichton was in the Cipher Department during the war."

"Was he?" Deborah blinked at this sudden change of subject. "I should suppose he wished to continue to be of service, even after his injury."

"He mentioned this to Perry when they discussed the mystery rhyme—the one found in the *vicomtesse*'s old desk."

Deborah did not immediately respond. The doggerel had been in her own thoughts, though she had spoken of it to no one. For a visitor, Simon Trewin was remarkably well-informed.

Still, she recalled, Tante Louise had said the discovery had been the talk of the village. Trewin must have heard of it in some local gossip.

"Perry is very taken with the notion of lost treasure," she said lightly.

"And you, Miss Stormont? What is your own view?"

Again Deborah paused before replying. She had her own ideas, but she was not ready to discuss them—not now and not with Simon Trewin. Instead, she smiled. "I thought we had agreed that it was an altogether fantastical notion, Dr. Trewin."

Trewin did not return her smile. "I wonder if Crichton thinks so."

Deborah felt her exasperation growing. Simon seemed obsessed with Lord Crichton this morning! "As I said before," she repeated tartly, "his lordship's opinions are best discussed with his lordship."

Trewin did not answer. He had bent over and plucked a blade of grass. He twisted it between his fingers, frowning. She had the impression that he was thinking how best to frame his next remark.

"I believe," he said hesitantly, "and here my informant is again your brother, that there is an engagement between Lord Crichton and Miss Phipps-Hedder?"

"I am not in his lordship's confidence," said Deborah stiffly, "though I collect that you are correct. However, since such an engagement is not yet official, it is scarcely a proper subject for public discussion."

"Quite, quite. But pray, bear with me, Miss Stormont. I have your best interests at heart, I do assure you."

"Then I wish you will be somewhat clearer, sir, for I confess that I am entirely at sea as to what you aim at here."

"Very well." Trewin tossed the grass aside. "In view of that engagement, I have asked myself why his lordship has not removed to the château."

Deborah sighed. "Dr. Trewin, I can only repeat that Lord Crichton's affairs are his own." *And I only wish,* she thought wryly, *that he might hear me say so!*

"But he may have other reasons . . . reasons beyond the personal. . . ."

Deborah was now definitely irritated. She reached for her reticule. "Lord Crichton's reasons cannot concern me, sir." *Nor you,* her tone implied.

"But they may. They may, indeed." Trewin spoke earnestly, leaning forward. "I am not simply gossip-mongering, Miss Stormont. I have been thinking. Crichton is a cipher-master. He has free access both here and at the château. Peregrine told me his lordship was most interested in that rhyme. And now—" he paused "—now he has made this completely unexpected journey to Rennes. Miss Stormont, is it not possible that Crichton has seen something in this rhyme and now wishes to secure the treasure for himself?"

The colour flared in Debs's cheeks. "I'll not believe it! What can have given you such a notion?"

Trewin glanced away from her flushed face and challenging eyes. "I have given you my reasons, Miss Stormont. And . . . I had such a strange conversation with him. I had mentioned this piece of verse, in jest, you know, when suddenly his tone became decidedly menacing. Why, Miss Stormont, it was as though he were warning me off!''

"You must have mistaken the matter, sir." Deborah had regained control of herself. "You have refined too much upon a passing remark. Let us now, I pray you, speak of some other matter." Her tone brooked no contradiction. "His lordship, I am persuaded, is the soul of probity and may well manage his own affairs."

She did not think that Simon Trewin was satisfied, but she had given him little choice. Courteously, he nodded his head at her request.

"As you wish, Miss Stormont. Will you tell me what you have found to draw recently?"

Deborah was glad of the change of topic, but she had found the whole exchange highly disturbing. She was relieved when Trewin shortly took his leave. She sat still, biting her lower lip. She wished Simon Trewin had not come that day.

Lord Crichton could not have seen anything in that rhyme. And, after all, what could there be to see? She had gone over and over it in her own mind and still caught no glimmer of meaning.

Deborah stopped and made a face. *Now* who was being fantastical? She would be babbling like Gwendolyn Phipps-Hedder next!

"Afternoon, Deborah." Freddie dropped onto the bench beside her. Perry joined him with a dissatisfied grunt.

She looked at their dejected faces. "What's happened?" she asked.

"Nothing," Perry said disgustedly. "Nothing. It was all a fizz."

"Nothing but that daisies-and-dandelions chap."

"Daisies and dand—do you mean Dr. Trewin?"

"Just him," Perry said. "Not someone after the Muscadet at all, just that botanizing ass."

"Oh, I say," Freddie protested, "I shouldn't call him an ass exactly. Though why he wants to traipse all over the place asking silly questions, I don't know."

"Should have brought Debs with us the last time." Perry scowled. "That innkeeper kept babbling *'Tray ween'* at us. She would have twigged right away that he was trying to say 'Trewin,' not—" he glared at his friend "—not chatting about the weather."

"The...the weather?" Debs was trying to look suitably serious.

Freddie was embarrassed. "Well, how was I to know he wasn't gassing on about how blustery it was? I told you I don't speak French." He appealed to Deborah. "*'Tray'* means something like 'a lot,' don't it?"

"Usually it means 'very,'" Debs murmured.

Perry snorted, emitting a sound that would have done justice to the Duchesse herself. "And you thought he was saying 'very windy'! To think we wasted our time on that when we could have been up at the château."

"Come on, old chap." Freddie got up. "Edouard promised us some ice-wine if we came over for tea. We can just make it, if we hurry."

"By George, yes!" Perry leapt up. "Come on!" He was halfway up the steps when he remembered his sister. "Do you care to join us, Debs?"

"N-no, thank you." Deborah's voice sounded rather strangled, but the young men were in too much of a hurry to notice. She waited till they were out of earshot before she finally burst into laughter.

"Oh dear," she whispered, wiping her eyes. "Very windy," indeed! She had quite forgotten her conversation with Simon and his doubts.

She simply longed to see Lord Crichton and tell him the *tray ween* story. She couldn't wait to see that little curl start at the side of his mouth and slowly grow into a full laugh.

How he would enjoy the joke! Quite restored to good humour, Deborah went back inside to ask her aunt exactly when Lord Crichton was expected to return.

And the footman, who had been detailed to watch her, heaved a sigh of relief and followed her into the house.

CHAPTER SIXTEEN

FRIDAY DAWNED CLEAR and bright and a collective sigh seemed to echo over the Bois. Peregrine leapt out of bed, dragged back the draperies and beamed as he saw the blue sky. It would have been, he thought, utterly intolerable if it had rained. He took up his coffee and then his eye fell on two tissue-wrapped parcels on his dressing-table. His cup halfway to his mouth, Perry fell into a most agreeable daydream.

Down another corridor, Madame d'Auray sipped chocolate and ran over last-minute details. Yes, she considered, everything was progressing well. Very well indeed, if one's thoughts turned a certain way....

How much she looked forward to seeing Deborah in that gown—and of course, one also wanted to see ...

Rapidly, Louise reviewed the miles between Beganne St. Pierre and Rennes. Yes, yes, highly satisfactory. Madame d'Auray, too, began to spin intriguing dreams.

Deborah was also drinking chocolate this morning. So the day had at last arrived! She had to admit that she was intensely curious about the gown. Tante Louise's taste was impeccable and she had never had a ball-gown before. She was excited and a little nervous.

How exactly did one go on at a ball? And wouldn't it be too embarrassing, if one actually lacked for partners? By a process of thought she did not care to examine too closely, Deborah's attention turned to Lord Crichton.

So surprising that he had suddenly left for Rennes. Business, her aunt had said rather vaguely. Debs couldn't imagine what sort of business that might be . . . something to do with his bankers, perhaps?

Simon Trewin had apparently seen something suspicious in that unexpected journey, but Deborah would have nothing to do with such reservations. If Lord Crichton had any information she was sure he must have spoken to Tante Louise.

But could he actually believe that little rhyme had anything to do with the treasure? He was a level-headed and thoughtful man. He would know that Madame d'Auray's explanation was the likeliest: the valuables had been brought to Paris and lost in the turmoil there.

Long-lost treasure might well appeal to Gwendolyn and Perry. But in the cold light of day and reason it was harder to accept. Uncle Raoul and the *vicomte* had apparently delighted in all kinds of puzzles and puns. Wasn't it likely that the finger rhyme was one of these games?

Still, Deborah was reluctant to accept her own arguments completely. The last line, for instance: "everything is yours." Didn't that suggest . . . Deborah shook herself. She must not let herself be carried away by such speculations, however entrancing they might be.

No, the best thing she could do would be to sound out Beron later, when he returned. And that return, she trusted, wouldn't be too much longer.

Indeed, when she spoke to her aunt, Louise was confident that Lord Crichton would be back in good time for the ball. And that, Deborah thought, with a sudden drop of spirits, must be a great relief to Miss Phipps-Hedder. Naturally, the prospect of dancing with his future fiancée would spur his return.

Abruptly Deborah put down her chocolate. It seemed bitter this morning. She pushed aside the tray and climbed down the bed steps. She must not mope about all morning.

Going to the huge dark wood wardrobe, she chose a rather severe navy blue gown. Then she sat down before the looking-glass and did her own hair. When Marie-Claire arrived and cried out against such sobriety, Deborah said shortly that tonight would be time enough for frivolity.

As LUCK WOULD HAVE IT, Miss Stormont was the first person to see Lord Crichton upon his return to the Bois. He blinked a little at the sober aspect she presented.

"Good morning, Miss Stormont," he muttered. "You are quite recovered now, I take it?"

Deborah stared at him. She had forgotten her accident. "Oh!" she said and then, "Oh, yes, I'm perfectly well, my lord."

She didn't look it, Beron thought. She was decidedly pale, though perhaps that was owing to the very dark colour of her dress—and her hair. Why, it was perilously close to that dreadful style she had been used to wear. He gave her a dubious glance, hoping this was not a portent for this evening.

For a moment, he wondered if he'd been on a fool's errand. But at least she had survived his absence without further mishap. He became aware that Deborah was speaking.

"...back in time, Miss Phipps-Hedder, I am persuaded, must have been overwhelmed by disappointment."

"Eh?" Now it was Lord Crichton's turn to stare blankly.

A faint flush crept over Deborah's throat and cheeks, which appeared very white against the dark gown. Surely he couldn't construe such a conventional remark as interference in his affairs?

"Ah!" His lordship nodded brusquely, as if just recalling his intended bride. "Miss Phipps-Hedder. Just so."

His tones struck Deborah as unencouraging, and as usual, she retreated to formality. "Have you taken luncheon yet, my lord? I shall tell Bigard to set something out for you, if you so desire."

This was clearly not the time to speak about the mysterious rhyme. His opinion of her had never been high and to evidence any degree of credence in such skimble-skamble stuff must sink her beyond reproach.

"Thank you, Miss Stormont." Lord Crichton was equally distant. "I should be glad of that."

Deborah inclined her head and set off to find the butler. Shrugging his shoulders slightly, Lord Crichton made his way upstairs to change. Both of them felt considerably put out that their meeting should have been so different from what had been anticipated.

THOUGH THERE WERE those at the Bois who considered that the afternoon and early evening dragged on interminably, to Deborah it was almost too soon that she stood in her shift, waiting.

"Here it is!" Louise appeared with her arms full and reverently laid her burden across Deborah's bed.

Debs caught her breath. Somewhat tentatively, she reached out a hand and touched the shimmering cloth. It was a deep rose colour, the satin flowing almost like liquid into the elegant Grecian lines. It was perfectly simple—nothing but the column of gorgeous colour.

"Yes," Madame d'Auray eyed it with deep satisfaction. "Marie-Claire and I had many discussions about roses and trimmings and netting. But, in the end, we decided the satin needed no enhancement."

"No, no, it is perfection as it is." Deborah looked up as the maid came in. "You and my aunt have worked wonders, Marie-Claire."

"And these we have made for your hair, *mademoiselle.*" She beamed and laid two roses of the same satin and a matching ribbon beside the gown.

Almost in a trance, Deborah allowed herself to be dressed. Marie-Claire refused to permit her to look in the pier-glass till her hair was done.

"*Mais non!*" she declared, vigorously wielding a hairbrush. "*Non! Non!* You must wait for the whole effect."

"I am in your hands," Deborah told her, smiling. "Carry on, Marie-Claire!"

But when she was finally granted a look at herself, Deborah could only stand still and slowly shake her head.

"You do not like it!" Marie-Claire wailed.

"Not like it!" Deborah turned, watching as the rose-pink folds flowed with her. "How could I not like it? It's just...just that I've never had a dress like this before...never looked like this before." She touched a hand to the shining mass of curls piled on her head. The velvet ribbon was threaded through them, anchored above her right ear with the two satin roses.

"Excellent, simply excellent." Madame d'Auray reappeared. She herself was very grand in dove grey figured silk with diamond combs in her white hair. "And I have brought you just the things to finish it off to perfection."

Deborah saw that her aunt was carrying a small japanned tray with a selection of parcels done in white tissue and tied up with gold thread.

"What are these, Tante Louise?"

"But naturally we have thought to give you a little present, my dear. Take one, do."

Deborah unwrapped the nearest parcel. It was a tiny handkerchief of lace-trimmed cambric, dyed to match her gown. "From Freddie," she said, reading from the card.

"Most appropriate." Madame d'Auray handed her the next parcel. "Now this one is from Perry."

"Perry? How thoughtful of him. And do look! Isn't it delightful?" She held up the silver mesh reticule with a pink silk cord.

"Just the thing for tonight. And here, my dear, this was delivered this afternoon, with Dr. Trewin's compliments."

"Simon Trewin!" Deborah stopped unwrapping. "But why? I mean—"

"My dear, if you were in London, or even Paris as I knew it, it would be quite à la modality for beaux to send you trinkets, especially before a ball."

"We-e-el." Deborah was still doubtful. "If you say it is quite proper—"

"My dear Debs, there are no scandal-mongers from Almack's here, and I am persuaded that Dr. Trewin has not overstepped the bounds of propriety. There!" she exclaimed as Deborah held up a fan. "Completely unexceptionable."

"But very pretty." Deborah opened and closed the pink-painted sticks.

"Slip the ribbon over your wrist," Louise advised her, "so that it will be at hand, should you require it. Now this—" she put another tissue-tied bundle into her niece's hand "—is from me."

"But, Tante, you have already given me the gown. You shouldn't—"

"Oh, pooh, child. I wanted to—"

"Tante Louise!" Reverently Debs held the two ear-rings of tiny pearl clusters in her hand. "They are so, so perfect." She leaned over and kissed her aunt. "And they have a pink tone, too."

"There, there, you absurd child! You must not cry." Louise's own voice was husky. "Take Freddie's handkerchief and dry your eyes."

"Seems a shame to use it for such a mundane purpose."

"Don't forget you've got one more parcel here. Open this and we shall be on our way."

"But who can this be from?"

"Why, Lord Crichton, of course."

"Lord Crichton! But I couldn't possibly..."

"Now Debs," said Louise briskly. "Don't be missish. Lord Crichton is a man of the world. He knows how such matters are arranged."

Wordlessly, Deborah held out a box.

As she took it, Madame d'Auray's eyebrows rose. A little something, his lordship had said, a string of pearls, a trifle like that. Gently, Louise let the necklace run through her fingers. The pearls were perfectly matched as to size and colour, all shimmering with the same rosy iridescence.

"Yes, they are lovely, are they not? He asked my advice and I told him a necklet would be very acceptable."

"B-but where can he have got them here? And they must be frightfully expensive...."

Madame d'Auray was sure that they were and that Lord Crichton must have scoured Rennes for his "suitable little trinket." That knowledge was giving her furiously to think.

"Now, *ma chère*," she said aloud. "Just turn around and let me fasten these for you."

"But Tante, I can't! I mean, surely I mustn't—"

"Deborah, surely we are not going to be so vulgar as to refuse a gift because of its price?"

"N-n-no, but—"

"You will accept Lord Crichton's gift as you have all the others. Let us go down and you may thank everyone yourself." She turned Deborah back towards the pier-glass. "See how delightfully you look."

Privately, Madame d'Auray considered that the girl was breathtakingly beautiful. It would be hard to say whether the pearls had given her their own shimmer or whether they had simply taken on their owner's rosy glow.

"Come along," she said. "Let us go." *And let us,* she said to herself, *let us see how a certain two gentlemen react.*

Still almost in a dream, Deborah floated downstairs to where Perry, Freddie and Lord Crichton were waiting. It was almost, she thought as she accepted their compliments, as though they were speaking to someone else, someone who was not really Deborah Stormont. Then, as she shyly thanked Lord Crichton for his gift, she suddenly looked deep into his eyes.

He admired her. She couldn't be mistaken in that look. He wasn't looking at her as though she were a country sloven. He was looking at her as though she were a pretty—no, a *beautiful*—woman.

The bubble of happiness which surrounded Deborah grew. She gave Lord Crichton a brilliant smile and allowed him to hand her into the carriage. What a wonderful evening it was going to be!

Manoeuvring himself into a seat across from Miss Stormont so that he might unobtrusively study her, Lord Crichton congratulated himself. He'd always known she'd be a beauty. By Jove, she'd have them on their ears in Almack's, if they could see her now.

No trace of that dowdy, schoolmistress figure he'd first met on the Dover Road. Those pearls were a dashed good idea of his. They had nothing on the lustre of that skin, though.

What, he asked himself, would she look like in other jewels? Not diamonds for that colouring, of course—coloured stones—emeralds or rubies—yes, rubies on those long, elegant fingers. . . .

Lord Crichton settled back in his seat. This was one ball he was going to enjoy.

CHAPTER SEVENTEEN

By London standards, the supper dance at the Château de Keroualles was a small affair. But to the majority of the guests it was an event of great social importance. Certainly Miss Deborah Stormont considered it a glittering occasion.

She was dancing for the second time with Simon Trewin, and there was no mistaking the admiration in that gentleman's eyes.

"It is a great relief to see that you have suffered no lasting ill effects from that unhappy accident," he said with a warm glance.

Deborah tossed her glossy curls. "I really cannot think how I came to be so foolish as to knock myself out."

"Perhaps you were somewhat distracted," Trewin suggested.

"By thoughts of the treasure, do you mean?" Debs chuckled. "Perry thinks so. According to him, the treasure-hunters went mad and attacked me. I'm afraid he found what he considered suspicious signs at the menhirs and that encouraged him enormously."

Trewin swung her swiftly into a turn. "Suspicious signs? Empty chests, perhaps? A few gold guineas? Or was there a feather from the pirate's parrot?"

Deborah laughed. "Nothing so exciting. Perry thought someone had been digging, but I suspect it was some animal in search of food rather than pieces of eight."

They twirled past Lord Crichton who was escorting one of the local young ladies. He frowned slightly as the other couple danced past. It was distasteful to see Miss Stormont flirting so outrageously with Simon Trewin.

Lord Crichton's view of the ball was rapidly souring. When he had first heard of it, he had thought the ball would be the ideal time to make a formal proposal to Gwendolyn. The matter had, he considered, dragged on long enough. It was time the whole thing was settled. It did not occur to him that this was a most unlover-like attitude and he did not examine why he should want a conclusion so badly.

He took leave of his partner, still struck dumb at the thought of having actually danced with the English milord, and looked about him. His frown grew as he saw that Simon Trewin had fetched a glass of champagne for Miss Stormont and they were laughing together as they drank.

He had greeted Gwendolyn in the reception line but he had not seen her since. He glanced over the dance floor again, then strode off towards the supper room.

Out of the corner of her eye, Deborah saw him go and guessed the reason. She sighed a little. Naturally he was more interested in dancing with Gwendolyn than with her.

"Debs! Debs!" Freddie Wimpole hastened up. "Debs, may I speak to you for a few moments, please?"

"I shall see if Mam'zelle de Keroualle may find a space for me on her dance card. I'll dare to hope for another dance later, Miss Stormont." Trewin bowed and departed.

Freddie watched him with an inimical look. He still had not forgiven Trewin for being the mysterious stranger.

"Now, Freddie," Deborah said, recalling his attention. "What is the matter? You look positively distracted."

Freddie took her arm. "Can't talk here," he said, "come outside. They've opened the doors to the garden." He led her onto the wide terrace and over to a small stone bench, overshadowed by a huge hydrangea bush.

It was a beautiful, warm night, Deborah thought, looking around in pleasure. Overhead was a harvest moon, full and golden in the dark blue sky.

Freddie sat beside her, scuffling his feet in the white marble chips on the pathway.

"Tell me, Freddie," she urged. "What is on your mind?"

"Dashed delicate matter," he muttered. "But—well, have you seen Beron lately?"

"He was in the ballroom, but I saw him leave. But don't you think, Freddie—" Deborah paused for a moment "—that he may be with Miss Phipps-Hedder?"

Freddie sighed and tugged at his cravat.

Deborah had a sudden premonition. "Goodness!" she gasped. "You're not, that is, you don't care for Miss Phipps-Hedder yourself, do you?"

"Yes, that is, no." Freddie grinned fleetingly. "But not the Miss Phipps-Hedder, you know. It's Jennifer I care for."

"Jennifer?"

"Younger sister," Freddie affirmed. "But the Phipps-Hedders are high-sticklers. Can't have a younger sister married first. Besides, Jen ain't properly out yet, not till next year."

"But Freddie, isn't Gwendolyn to be married soon? I cannot say whether Sir Rodney will approve your suit, but surely her marriage will remove one obstacle?"

Freddie kicked a chip and watched it tumble down to the lawn. "Debs," he began, "you seem to get along all right with Beron. Does he strike you as a man in love?"

"I'm sure Lord Crichton's feelings are all that they ought to be," Deborah returned stiffly.

Freddie sighed again and kicked another pebble. "I mean, it's jam for me if Gwen gets off—the earlier the better, actually. But Beron is a friend of mine, after all, and—"

"Freddie, what is all this? What are you trying to say?"

Mr. Wimpole froze, then pointed. Deborah followed his finger. A couple were crossing the lawn. They walked close together, arm-in-arm. The moonlight shone on dark hair and soft brown curls. Then the two vanished into the shadows of the Allée.

"Gwendolyn and Edouard de Keroualle!" Deborah gasped. "I did wonder..."

Freddie groaned and sank back. "Gwendolyn!" he said clutching his head. "She looks like a harmless enough chit, but once she's away from her mama there's no holding her."

"Freddie! You cannot mean that they are eloping!"

"Won't elope," Freddie said gloomily. "Got a conventional streak in her, wouldn't risk the scandal of Gretna Green. Jen, now..." He brightened up. "Jen's pluck to the backbone. She's a real—"

"I don't doubt that Miss Jennifer is a lady of rare quality," Deborah said with asperity. "But it is Gwendolyn we have to deal with now. If she is not eloping, what is she doing?"

"One night of bliss."

"I beg your pardon, Freddie!"

"One night of bliss—it's some of that frightful tosh she reads. This one's all about some wretched girl who has only one night to say farewell to the man she loves before her cruel parents marry her off to someone else."

"What sentimental nonsense!"

"I should say so, but Gwendolyn likes that sort of stuff."

"Does she mean to refuse Lord Crichton, then?" Deborah demanded more sharply than she had intended.

"Won't do that." Freddie shook his head. "Hasn't the bottom for it. Won't defy old Huff-and-Gruff. Sees herself as the persecuted heroine of one of these romances."

"Then she intends to marry Lord Crichton, even though she cares nothing for him?" Deborah could not keep the horror out of her voice.

Freddie looked surprised. "Done all the time in Society, ain't it?"

Deborah got up and began to stride up and down, pounding her clenched fist into her palm.

"Thing is," Freddie said, "I've been wondering about Beron. I thought that he was getting . . . I mean, I thought he might be . . . That is, you and he . . ." Freddie floundered helplessly.

Miss Stormont paid no attention to this. "But what can we do?" she demanded. "We can't just stand by while he walks into a loveless marriage—"

Freddie looked up in alarm. "Here! Beron won't thank us for interferin' in his affairs."

Deborah stopped, the memory of another scene fresh in her mind. "No, no, he certainly wouldn't. But what can we do?"

Freddie got up. "We can make sure he don't find that widgeon Gwendolyn and Edouard in some compromising situation. This ain't one of her novels, after all, and a scene at a ball wouldn't be good ton. Not," he corrected himself, "not that Beron's ton ain't always good, but still—"

"Oh, yes! It would be dreadful if he should stumble across them accidentally. Miss Phipps-Hedder herself must speak to him. He cannot find out in this way."

"Right." Freddie had become more decisive. "I'll go back inside, see if I can head him off to the card-room. You stay out here, in case he should take it into his head to get some air. Above all," Freddie added, directing a glare towards the Allée, "don't let those priceless idiots come back into the ballroom together."

"I shall not," Deborah promised fervently. "Do go, Freddie. Every moment now I dread to see Lord Crichton appear."

"He won't if I can help it." Freddie hurried off.

Deborah sank down on the bench, her mind in a whirl. She had seen there was an attraction between the young *vicomte* and Miss Phipps-Hedder. But she had thought—hoped—it was merely a harmless flirtation. She had not imagined that Gwendolyn's affections were truly engaged. No wonder the *vicomte* sometimes looked so black. But why didn't they appeal to Sir Rodney....

Deborah caught herself up. Of course: the *vicomte* had no fortune. Whatever money there was must be devoted to the upkeep of the château. If it came to a choice between Edouard and Lord Crichton, Sir Rodney's decision must be obvious.

Money! Deborah struck her fist against the stone seat. What problems it created. For Perry and Julie and now for Edouard and Gwendolyn.

There was a quick footstep behind her and Deborah gasped as she beheld Lord Crichton.

Beron was not in the best of tempers. He had thought he had seen Gwendolyn in the supper room, but Julie de Keroualle had accosted him and kept him chatting. By the time he managed to escape, Gwendolyn had vanished.

He'd gone back to the dance floor and there Freddie had found him. Mr. Wimpole had been intent on inveigling him into the card-room. At one point, he'd thought Freddie was actually going to try dragging him there. His lordship had almost been obliged to be rude, and it was only a young lady's claiming Freddie for a dance which had allowed Beron to get away at all.

Now he found himself confronting Miss Stormont. The moonlight, he noticed, was creating intriguing shadows in the hollows of her throat and shoulders. Impatiently, he dismissed this thought.

Instead, he frowned at her and almost bit off the words. "Good evening, Miss Stormont. May I ask if you have seen Miss Phipps-Hedder?"

"Oh, er . . ." Deborah looked vaguely about, as though she expected to see Gwendolyn emerge from the hydrangea bush. "She's not here," she said brightly.

"I can see that, Miss Stormont." His voice dropped dangerously. "I enquired if you'd seen her."

"Yes, I saw her, and very lovely she looked, too." Deborah tried to sound natural. She forced herself to stare straight ahead. She must not look towards the Allée at all. If only Gwendolyn and Edouard did not suddenly appear on that disastrously bright lawn! "Yes." She smiled artificially. "That shade of mint green suits her prodigiously, does it not? Especially with those sleeves cut à la—"

"Miss Stormont, I did not ask for a dissertation on female fashion." He stared challengingly at Deborah. Lord Crichton was beginning to suspect a conspiracy: a conspiracy to keep him from Miss Phipps-Hedder.

Deborah longed to turn around, just to glance into that darkness where the Allée began. She felt Beron's accusing glare, and infuriatingly, she felt her face begin to flush.

Desperately, she tried to think of something to say. In the silence, from beyond the lawn, a feminine giggle echoed. Both Lord Crichton and Miss Stormont swung round.

Beron smiled. "I see. Miss Phipps-Hedder and some of the young ladies have gone for a stroll." His smile broadened. "Their duennas may not approve, but I assure you, Miss Stormont, that I shall not squeak beef." He looked more kindly at her.

A good sport, he thought, trying to keep the girls out of trouble. But she didn't seem reassured. She was still staring at him with those huge black eyes. Funny how the moonlight and shadows seemed to chase each other about that little hollow in her throat....

"Ahem!" Lord Crichton straightened up. "I think," he said casually, "I shall just walk down and meet the young ladies."

"Oh, no!" Deborah jumped. "Don't do that, my lord."

He raised an eyebrow. "But I have told you I do not intend to carry tales, Miss Stormont."

"Yes, that is, no. I am persuaded, my lord, that they, that is, that Miss Phipps-Hedder will return directly. Would you care to take a turn about the terrace, my lord? There are some delightful vistas on the other side of the house."

"Thank you, Miss Stormont, but as I said, I believe I will walk down the lawn." All Beron's suspicions returned.

"No, no!" Deborah threw caution to the winds. "Please, my lord. I assure you it will be better to stay here."

Beron's frustrations now boiled over. He glared at her. How dared she stand there, looking a moon gold sprite and determined—*again*—to manage his affairs.

"I thank you for your advice, Miss Stormont." His eyes glittered in the moonlight. "But I believe I may dispense with it." He turned on his heel and took the steps two at a time.

Deborah stared after him, then she rushed inside to find Freddie.

Lord Crichton strode furiously on. Really, the Stormont female had gone too far this time! But he would permit no interference. He was going to propose to Gwendolyn Phipps-Hedder and no one was going to stop him.

He had crossed the grass and now stared about him. The woods bordered the lawn here and surely young ladies with ball-gowns would not— Ah! He had forgotten the Allée des Chênes.

Beron smiled indulgently. Probably it was exactly the sort of romantic venue that would appeal to girls who had slipped their leash. It was dark under the trees, however, and the underlay of leaves muffled his footsteps. He was mildly surprised to find the Allée so badly lit. Perhaps he ought to mention to Gwendolyn and her friends that it might not be entirely wise to wander such places at night.

But it was getting brighter now. He was approaching the clearing; the trees were thinning and the moonlight was streaming brightly down.

Lord Crichton stopped. He had found Miss Phipps-Hedder. But she was not surrounded by a bevy of giggling girls. Nor was she alone. She was locked in a passionate embrace with the Vicomte de Keroualle and both of them were oblivious to anything else.

Beron turned and left as silently as he had come.

CHAPTER EIGHTEEN

THERE WERE at least two people at the Bois to whom sleep did not come easily that night. The rose satin gown had been carefully put away. The pearls and ear-rings had been laid in their velvet box. The dance card had been safely stowed for a nostalgic remembrance.

Deborah herself was in bed, but she was not asleep. The night was warm and she had pulled back the draperies so that the moonlight trailed a wide ribbon of golden light across the bedroom floor.

But Miss Stormont could not leave the events of the night. What had happened after she had left the terrace? Had Lord Crichton seen Gwendolyn and Edouard?

The young couple had at last returned to the ballroom. At least, Deborah thought, they had had the sense not to reappear together.

She and Freddie had lingered on the terrace, eventually attracting disapproving stares themselves. Lord Crichton had, in due course, turned up in the card-room where he had played competently and genially till the ball concluded shortly after one o'clock.

He had not said much in the coach on the way back to the Bois. But then, Deborah reflected, Perry had talked so much that no one else had had the opportunity to say anything at all.

But why was she going over and over all this? It was not her affair. She must try to think of something else.

Failing signally in this endeavour, Miss Stormont tossed back the sheets. It wasn't doing any good to lie here. She felt for the steps with her bare feet and crossed over to the window.

Looking out, she saw the poplars cast long black shadows across the moonlit lawns. Something moved in Deborah's mind... some memory... some similarity....

She tried to pin down the elusive thought. Was it something she had drawn? In one of her sketches? She went to the table and reached for her sketch-book. But it was not there.

She searched swiftly through the drawers, then the other places in the room. But there was no satchel or sketch-book there. She sat down to think.

Where had she seen them last? The last sketch she'd done had been of that purple plant—the one she'd asked Simon Trewin about. Yes, she remembered riffling through the book as she'd talked to him that day by the *étang*. Then she'd packed up and gone to see the giant stones.

Deborah had a sudden vivid vision of the megalith field in the bright sunlight. She saw the huge grey stones, their shadows dark behind them and, in front of her, the long, thin shadow of the pine tree.

She sat very still. It was not just the sketch she was remembering. It was an idea....

But how absurd! It must have been the sun. It had addled her brain! She took a few agitated steps. It was a lunatic notion, but—*but*— Her excitement was growing: could it possibly be true?

She paused by the window again. Yes, it was a clear, bright night, the trees' shadows pointing long and dark across the moonlit lawn. She would, yes, she *would* go and see for herself!

It was, of course, a completely ridiculous notion, or so Deborah told herself as she made a quick toilette. Ridiculous, but she was going to test it!

She slipped out of her room and down the stairs. Some steps creaked frighteningly loudly. She paused, listening intently, but there was no sign anyone else had been disturbed.

She tiptoed down the front hall and turned towards the kitchen hall to a little garden door. The bolts slid easily back and now she was outside in the herb garden. The moonlight was still bright and it was quite easy to see her way.

She came out below the terrace, went past the silent fountain and out onto the path to the *étang*.

The Duchesse was sleeping peacefully under some currant bushes. She stared at Deborah with her strange liquid gaze, yawned and shut her eyes again.

"Good night, your grace," Debs said softly and quickened her pace. It was exhilarating to be out alone at such an hour. She chuckled as she thought that no one could call this venture in any way sensible.

All about her was very quiet, but there were soft little scurryings in the grass. She was quite unafraid, even at the occasional louder sound. She cocked her head and listened; it was only animals, she concluded hopefully.

But any nervousness would have been overridden by her excitement. It was a ludicrous idea, but... But suppose, just suppose, it happened to be true! It wasn't possible; she didn't believe it, but... but...

Deborah passed quickly through the poplar stand, their leaves whispering softly to her in the night air and came out to see the *étang* glimmering in the moonlight. She circled it swiftly and plunged into the pine wood.

It was much darker in there, and Debs began to look more fearfully about her. The noises seemed to have increased significantly. She hurried on, her feet stumbling on stones and small holes and the branches pulling at her clothes.

But at last she was out of the wood. The clear yellow moonlight shone down on the field of huge grey stones. Deborah put her hand on the bole of the single pine and studied the field.

The evergreen threw one straight, long shadow ahead, the top of which fell squarely over an upright megalith in the third row. Their shapes echoed each other, she thought, her heart thumping. They were just like fingers, fingers reaching . . .

Suddenly the curtain in her mind lifted and she saw the scene as she'd seen it before—but that time in sunlight, not moonlight. Memory flooded back. She gazed upwards, but even as she stretched her arms to their highest, she could not touch the lowest branch.

"Just so, Miss Stormont."

Deborah gasped and whirled round.

Lord Crichton detached himself from the shadows of the wood and strolled towards her. "Good evening, or better, good morning, Miss Stormont," he said, bowing as though they were meeting in the drawing-room before dinner.

"Wha-what," Debs stammered at him, "what are you . . . how did you—"

"I was not asleep and I heard the stairs outside my door creak most damnably. When I opened my door, I saw you vanishing down to the hall. So," he said with a shrug, "I followed. I cannot find it altogether *de rigueur* for young ladies to go out alone for rambles in the moonlight, however romantic the notion may seem."

"It is not a romantic ramble." She glanced upwards again and involuntarily shuddered.

"No," agreed Lord Crichton with a change of tone. He followed her gaze. "Whatever hit your head, it was not a pine branch."

Deborah had recovered her poise. "No, I see that. But what could it have been? I am not so poor-spirited as to come over faint for no reason at all. I was standing here, I turned round—"

"Why?"

It was casually said and she answered without needing to think. "I heard something—" She stopped and her eyes widened. "You mean . . . someone hit me?"

"Why?" Again it was the same conversational tone.

"But there can be no reason. I had nothing anyone could be interested in stealing. I had only my satchel with me."

"There was no satchel here when I found you, Miss Stormont." His lordship was watching her intently, almost as if he were willing her to think, to remember.

"But why?" she asked. "What could anyone want with a lot of sketches of plants—"

"And of megaliths."

"Yes, yes! And that's what I've remembered. In my sketches the stones looked like hands, like fingers reaching up out of the ground. I'd forgotten that, till I saw the poplar shadows on the lawn tonight. Then I remembered that day at the megaliths. I'd been looking at the pine tree, thinking how its shadow was like a long, pointing finger—and then I thought of the rhyme—"

"Quand le doigt est sur le doigt," Lord Crichton quoted. "The artist's eye. Yes, I thought it must be something like that, even if you couldn't remember. Raoul and

the *vicomte* must have seen the same resemblance to fingers as you had."

"So it was not really a cipher, after all."

"More like a kind of personal reference. Look," he said, pointing past her. "The shadow finger is on the stone finger."

Deborah stepped closer and clutched at his arm. "Do you think that the treasure is actually there?"

"It may have been," Beron said. "But you must remember there is no guarantee that it is still there after all this time. And, of course, they may never have had the opportunity to place it there."

"Let's see! Let's dig and see!"

Lord Crichton laughed. "Not with my bare hands." He reached behind him and produced a spade. "The Duchesse was highly incensed at my borrowing this, but I thought it might come in handy. I, too, have been thinking of prowlers and diggings and young ladies knocked senseless and anything at all that might be described as a finger."

Deborah laughed and pulled him out into the field. Her exhilaration had returned and she almost danced over to the stone. "There is no sign here of the digging Perry saw."

"There are over two hundred stones." Lord Crichton was shrugging out of his coat. "I suspect someone was testing your insight about fingers. But it would be a daunting task to excavate every stone. However, since we believe we have the clue, let us get to work!" He grasped the spade.

Deborah watched as he dug. The muscles rippled across his back and shoulders as he bent and straightened. It seemed very quiet except for Lord Crichton's breathing, and the time seemed to stretch on forever. Then, echoing loudly in the silence, the spade struck on something.

"What is it?" Deborah whispered.

Lord Crichton flashed her a quick grin, then worked more quickly, shovelling out the soft brown clay. Then he grunted in satisfaction, tossed aside the spade, bent down and heaved a large, wooden, earth-stained chest. Apparently it had once been covered in leather, but that now hung in tatters.

They both crouched beside it. "Can we open it?" Deborah breathed.

"The metal is worn and rusted." Lord Crichton's dark grey eyes were alight with the same excitement. "So I think..." He took the lock in his hands and wrenched it hard. There was a reluctant click and the padlock came away in two pieces.

Beron touched Debs's hand lightly, then raised the protesting lid.

At first, Deborah could see nothing. "Is it—" her voice almost broke "—is it empty?"

"Here." Beron leaned out into the full moonlight. He held a small brown leather bag. In the light, Debs recognized the d'Auray crest. Beron poured a stream of gold sovereigns into his hand. They glowed dully in the pale light.

Deborah reached for another bag. This time she recognized the arms from above the door of the château. The contents of this bag sparkled with an icy fire. "Diamonds!" she whispered. "So it was true. The *vicomte* and my uncle had gathered their valuables together."

"Quite right, my dear Miss Stormont, and I must thank you and Lord Crichton for finding them for me."

It was Simon Trewin. He had come from the other side of the field and now stood in front of them. The moonlight clearly illuminated the pistol held steadily in his hand and pointed directly at them.

Debs scrambled to her feet. "What does this mean, Dr. Trewin?" she demanded angrily.

"No, Miss Stormont." Lord Crichton rose more slowly, his eyes fixed on that pistol. "Whatever the fellow's name, it is not Trewin."

"So you know that, do you?" The newcomer smiled unpleasantly. "But it will do you little good." He gestured with the pistol. "Throw those bags back into the box, Miss Stormont, and shut it."

"I will not!" said Deborah hotly.

"I do not wish to shoot you, Miss Stormont, but if it becomes necessary, I shall not hesitate to do so."

Deborah looked at the gun, then over to Lord Crichton, who nodded almost imperceptibly. Flushing, she tossed the two bags back inside and slammed the lid of the box.

"I am obliged to you, Miss Stormont." He smiled mockingly. "That will make it so much easier for me."

Debs had stepped backwards toward Beron. She was about to respond indignantly when she felt his lordship's fingers pressing gently into her arm. She looked up and froze. A white shape had emerged from the woods and was advancing steadily upon the false Trewin.

"Do you think you'll get away with this?" Lord Crichton asked in his usual soft tones. Deborah realized he intended to keep the impostor's attention straight in front of him.

"Oh, I don't think so, my lord," the man sneered. "I know I shall."

Deborah saw that the Duchesse had stopped. Her right leg was lifted as she pawed the soft grass. "You'll never get away with it," she said loudly.

"But I shall, my dear Miss Stormont." He jerked his head slightly. "Over by the road my assistant is waiting with a coach with some extremely swift horses."

"That must be the lurking Gonidec," Beron murmured.

"Very clever, my lord, but I'm afraid I can no longer spare the time to continue this delightful conversat—" He looked away for a moment. A shout had come from the direction of the road.

But that diversion of attention was what the Duchesse had been waiting for. She snorted loudly, lowered her head and charged.

Her intended victim heard her, but before he could turn, her head contacted the seat of his pants. Once again he flew through the air, this time straight over the treasure box.

Beron pulled Deborah to one side as the false Trewin flew past them. With a sickening thud his head struck one of the menhirs and he collapsed, unconscious, on the grass.

Lord Crichton contemplated him for a moment, then turned to the Kashmir goat. "My congratulations, your grace," he said, and scratched one silky ear. The Duchesse sniffed and ate a dandelion.

Deborah looked at them and laughed shakily. "You're very cool, my lord."

Lord Crichton looked up, a smile playing about his generous mouth. "How should I be otherwise, with such examples before me?"

"Examples, sir?"

Beron gestured to her and to the Duchesse. "Anything less like a pair of vapourish females I have never seen."

Debs was about to make some rallying remark but she caught Beron's eye and the expression in those clear grey depths made her feel suddenly shy.

"Well, well, well," a new voice said, in tones of mild interest. "Can I have come upon an assignation?"

"Tante Louise!" gasped Deborah. "What are you doing here?"

"I might more reasonably ask you the same thing," her aunt replied, adjusting the demure lace cap that topped her astonishing Oriental dressing-gown. "What a good thing I decided to investigate all those creaking stairs."

Beron laughed. "We are not entirely compromised," he said, observing Deborah blush, "but—" he gestured towards the supine form "—one of our number may be said to have lost interest in the proceedings. Then again," he continued, patting Deborah's hand in an infuriating way, "I cannot think that any human chaperon would be as nice in her notions as the Duchesse." He went over to the unconscious man and took up his wrist.

"Good heavens!" gasped Madame d'Auray. "Can that be Dr. Trewin? Whatever has been happening?"

There was a crackle of twigs from the road side of the field and two figures came into the moonlight. Debs and Louise gaped and Lord Crichton remained unfazed.

"Ah, Freddie, Perry," he said as urbanely as if he welcomed them to his London house. "Good of you to join us."

"Is that you, Beron? Oh! Give you good evening, *madame,* Debs."

As the two young men came nearer, it was plain that they were in a state of high excitement. Their cheeks were red, their breathing ragged and their clothes disarranged.

Perry stared at the hole, box and spade. "What's going on here?" he enquired.

"Why don't you tell us what you have been doing first?" Lord Crichton laid down the unconscious man's hand and stood up. "What got you up, for instance?"

"Stairs creakin'," said Freddie promptly. "Didn't bother me the first time, but then it seemed like a whole troop of people were passin' through. After the third time, I got up to look." He bowed to Louise. "Saw you goin' downstairs, *madame*." He looked a trifle uneasy. "No right to interfere, of course, but when I saw you go out, well, what with these prowlers and that—well, I thought I'd best wake Perry." He shook his head. "Took the devil of a time to get him up and dressed. Couldn't see you anywhere when we got downstairs and out, *madame*. Peered about the garden, then decided to scout down the drive and along the road."

"And then," Perry burst in, "we saw a carriage stopped at the side of the road. Odd time for it to be there. So we went up. Saw the lamps were all covered. We were just staring at it—"

"When some fellow ambushed us!"

"Ambushed you!" Deborah and her aunt exclaimed in unison.

"Nothing to worry about," Perry said airily, smoothing back his cuffs. "Freddie and I took care of him, all right."

Freddie nodded complacently. "Left him trussed up in his own rope in his own carriage. Up to no good, of course, but we couldn't think what he might be about. Heard voices from this way, so thought we'd better check."

"Here!" Perry had been staring over at the form on the ground. "That's the roots-and-berries chap, ain't it? Trewin?"

"His name is not Trewin and I should doubt very much if he is truly a botanist," Beron told him. "At any rate it was not botany which brought him here tonight."

Perry was staring at the small chest. "Is that—"

"Yes, Perry." Debs took his arm. "It's the treasure!"

Louise's hand flew to her breast, but Perry dropped to his knees and flipped back the lid. He fumbled inside and impatiently shook out a brown bag. The sovereigns clinked and glowed in his hand.

"Oh, my dear boy! My dear Deborah!" Madame d'Auray took Deborah's hand and let her other hand rest on Perry's shoulder. "This is wonderful news for me and for you, my dearest children."

"But," Deborah protested, "we shouldn't, we cannot—"

"You are my family," her aunt said gently and firmly. "This good fortune is as much yours as mine and the *vicomtesse*'s."

Perry had been staring at the coins as though entranced. At these words he looked up. "The *vicomtesse!* Do you think—"

Louise lightly touched his cheek. "Yes, dear Perry. I do indeed think so."

Perry leapt up. "Julie!" he cried. "I must tell Julie!"

"Perry!" said Lord Crichton, catching him by the sleeve. "The *vicomtesse* may well be delighted to welcome you as a son-in-law, but not if you come barracking at her house at three o'clock in the morning."

"Not proper visiting hours," Freddie agreed. "Bad ton, old chap."

"Besides," his lordship went on, "I need your help. You've got one villain in that coach. I think his friend here had better join him."

"By Jove, yes!" Perry said. "Come on, Freddie. Let's get this precious pair locked up in the cellars of the Bois. Won't the magistrate get a jolt when we knock him up later this morning!"

"Such enthusiasm," his lordship sighed. "Could you perhaps wait a moment further? Your aunt should not be abroad in the damp air, so perhaps you will escort her home also?"

"Good idea," Freddie approved. "Delighted to be of service, ma'am."

His lordship bent and picked up the box. He dusted the last of the earth off it. Then with a bow, he presented it to Madame d'Auray. "This," he said, "belongs to you and the de Keroualles. You are the proper person to take charge of it."

Louise's eyes were bright in the moonlight. "I can never adequately express my gratitude to you, my lord."

"I merely followed Miss Stormont's lead," he said. Then his grey eyes held her black ones. "But I think you know the only reward which interests me."

Madame d'Auray blinked rapidly, then she said briskly, "Come along now, boys."

Between them Freddie and Perry heaved the now groaning false Trewin up, wrapped his arms about their shoulders and set off.

"Good night, my lord," Madame d'Auray said. "I shall send for the doctor as soon as I return home. Good night, my dear." She smiled at Deborah. "I'm sure Lord Crichton and, of course—" she glanced around at the goat browsing amongst the menhirs "—the Duchesse will look after you." And she set out after the others.

CHAPTER NINETEEN

"WELL!" Deborah stared as the others vanished around the stand of trees. "And I thought she was worried about my reputation!"

Lord Crichton was leaning back against a menhir, but that disturbing expression was back in his eyes. He said nothing, but his smile grew.

Deborah rushed into speech. "How did you know that man was not Trewin, my lord?"

"Ah, that was a fortunate coincidence. You see, I know Simon Trewin, the real one. He is indeed a botanist and an Oxford fellow, and I have been a friend of his since our schooldays. And," he added, "I shall speak to him as soon as I return to England. If he doesn't plan a compendium such as this villain suggested, then he certainly ought to. I promise you that your drawings will be published, anyway."

Deborah waved this aside. "You never told me he was an impostor," she said accusingly.

"I did not wish to tip him the wink. You are not an heiress, Miss Stormont, yet he had concocted this Banbury tale with the sole apparent purpose of getting close to you and your family. I thought I had best discover precisely what the object of such a masquerade might be."

"And it was the treasure." Deborah gazed at the hole. "But how came he to know of it?"

"Remember what Julie de Keroualle said: Gonidec had been in Oxford with them."

Quickly Deborah took the point. "And had been dismissed for prying into private papers."

"The French authorities will question both, of course. But I suspect that Gonidec had seen the old *vicomte*, Edouard's father, doing some of this treasure-gathering. When he realized the *vicomtesse* had not brought it with her to England, he began to look for clues as to its whereabouts."

"And he set up with this *soi-disant* Trewin while they were both in England."

"That seems likely. The impostor seemed familiar with the real Trewin, so I assume he had at least visited Oxford. But as you know, travel to France has been difficult for some years and furthermore, I think they may only recently have come upon your location."

"But when he got to Salisbury," Deborah said thoughtfully, "he found that we had removed to France."

"That must have confirmed his suspicions that you had some special information, so he followed you to France."

Deborah moved forward and began to scratch behind the Duchesse's ears. "And when I mentioned that the menhirs looked like hands, he immediately connected this to the rhyme."

"Rather, he believed that you had made a slip. I doubt he ever really credited the notion that none of you understood the rhyme. He had brooded over it for a long time and suspected that it dominated everyone else's thoughts, also. When you went to the menhir field directly after that remark about the stones, he must have thought you had the secret."

"The shadows!" Deborah put in. "I remember I could see the shadows clearly, but at the time I was only thinking of how the stones resembled fingers. I didn't connect them with the rhyme until tonight when I looked out and thought how the poplar shadows also looked like fingers."

"At that point our impostor was a little ahead of you. He didn't see the whole significance, but he did realize that the stones were the *doigts* of the rhyme. I expect he succumbed to panic, and tried to make sure you were the only one who had such knowledge."

"So he knocked me out and stole my satchel, in case anyone else interpreted my sketches in the same way."

"Yes, but he had to be careful about his investigations. He wasn't really sure where to look and I'm afraid I stirred Perry up and his searching of the menhir field kept the false Trewin away for a while. The famous *rôdeurs* were our self-proclaimed botanist and Gonidec, but after Perry's fervid speculations, they had to lie low."

"They must have been relieved that I could recall nothing of the attack on me."

Beron smiled slightly. "I emphasized that to him and I made light of the whole treasure business while I warned him, in what I flatter myself was a rather subtle way, that I had divined his plans. If he were innocent, the warning could mean nothing to him. If he were not, then it might add to his confusion."

"You *did* try to warn him! Why, he tried to warn *me*—against you!"

"And what did you make of that, my dear Miss Stormont?" Beron's tone was decidedly amused.

Deborah seemed to have found a burr in the Duchesse's coat. At any rate, something by the goat's ear claimed her full attention. She ducked her head and her voice came muffled back to him.

"Naturally I could not permit such presumption. Of course I refused to listen to such utter rubbish."

Lord Crichton laughed. "And yet he lives," he marvelled.

Miss Stormont regarded him warily over the Duchesse's back. She kept firmly to the subject at hand. "He was also Freddie's mysterious stranger and the questions he was asking had nothing to do with wine at all."

Beron laughed again. "He was after a greater prize than Muscadet, though Freddie might dispute that."

Deborah got to her feet. Somehow Lord Crichton had moved and she was taken aback to discover him standing disquietingly close to her. She stepped back a little. "Well," she said brightly, "it's all finished now. What a blessing that Perry will now be able to court Julie without compunction."

"Indeed," his lordship agreed courteously.

There was a silence.

"Well," Deborah said again. "Shall we return to the Bois, my lord?"

"Already?" Beron asked in surprise. "I was so enjoying the moonlight."

Deborah frowned. "You are pleased to be jocular, my lord. You wished my aunt out of the night air, so I presume you are aware that such air may induce a contagion of the lungs."

"But," said his lordship outrageously, "if I were to be so unlucky, I have no doubt that you would nurse me admirably."

"I should not!" Deborah responded immediately.

"Shouldn't you?" Lord Crichton's tones were soft but insistent. "Shouldn't you...Deborah?"

Miss Stormont's pulses raced and she had a sudden, almost overwhelming urge to hurl herself into his arms.

Sternly she suppressed such unseemly thoughts and endeavoured to give the conversation a more proper tone. "My lord, I must insist that we return at once. I could not reconcile it with my conscience if you were to catch a chill on my account."

"A managing female." Lord Crichton sighed. "I knew it the first moment I set eyes on you."

"Then I wonder you wish to remain here talking with me."

"Oh, talking wasn't what I had in mind."

Deborah blushed scarlet. "No—you can't! You mustn't! You are going to marry Miss Phipps-Hedder."

"No," said Beron calmly, "I'm not. If that hoard's going to smooth Perry's way, it is also going to make Edouard a more than acceptable *parti* for Gwendolyn."

Deborah spoke breathlessly, her eyes on his face. "Don't you . . . mind?"

"No, I don't. In fact," he said reflectively, "I don't think I ever would have married her, even if I had not discovered her partiality for Edouard."

"You wouldn't?" It was a small but very hopeful voice.

"No. You see—" he reached out and took her hand "—I have discovered that I prefer quite a different style of female."

Deborah studied the ground. His lordship reached over and tipped up her chin. "I discovered that while life with my particular kind of female might frequently be infuriating, life without her would be utterly unthinkable."

"No!" Deborah twisted away. "You mustn't. Oh, dear, how can you be so nonsensical?"

Beron's lips curved and that look in his eyes deepened. He took a step towards her, his hand outstretched.

Panic seized Miss Stormont and she stumbled sideways. His eyes still fixed on her face, Beron followed her.

But he stepped too close to the edge of the trench he had dug earlier. The side crumbled beneath his weight and Beron fell, his leg bending beneath him.

"Beron! Beron!" Deborah raced forward to clasp his arms. "Your leg! Your bad leg!"

Beron moaned and gripped her tighter.

"I can't, oh, I *can't* have done it again."

"But you have, my dear, indeed you have," he murmured faintly, his arms slipping about her neck.

"Can you move at all, dearest?" She bent solicitously over him. "If I pull, can you climb out?"

"I—I think so." His lordship made an effort to raise himself and Deborah helped him to crawl out onto the grass, where he lay with his head in her lap.

Gently, Deborah smoothed back the thick black hair. Beron sighed and closed his eyes. One hand lay along his leg, the fingers rubbing his knee.

"I am so sorry," Deborah said. "I never meant— Pray believe, I would never—" She stopped suddenly, her gaze riveted on those fingers. "Beron!" she cried in a strangled voice. "Beron!"

His lordship opened his eyes. "Yes?" he said weakly.

"You—you humbug!" Deborah sat up straighter. "That's your left leg. You were shot in your right leg. You've been bluffing me!" She wriggled out from under him.

Lord Crichton sat up and smiled into her indignant face. "Deplorable behaviour, isn't it?" he said without a shade of penitence.

"How dare you, my lord? How dare you?"

"'My lord'?" The dark eyebrows rose. "I thought we had made more progress in our acquaintance, Deborah?"

Miss Stormont ignored this deliberate provocation. "Why," she demanded, "why did you pretend that your leg was hurt?"

"Well," said his lordship reasonably, "it would be in keeping with the way you have been used to treat me, wouldn't it? I suppose I must congratulate myself that I have survived our courtship in one piece."

Deborah fell back against the nearest menhir. "Courtship?" she repeated incredulously. "Courtship?"

"An odd one, I do admit."

"Very odd, indeed." Deborah was beginning to recover herself. "If you have been conducting a courtship, my lord, it has been of Miss Phipps-Hedder, not me."

"And what a very lukewarm suitor she must have found me, to be sure." He gave a wry little smile that completely melted Miss Stormont's anger and went on, "You do have a point and I admit that it took me some time to recognize my own feelings. The question is now—" his gaze grew more intense "—have *you* recognized yours?"

Deborah's eyes fell. She stared at the tangle of grass and wild flowers beside her. Her chest rose and fell. "It's...it's not a proper question," she whispered.

"Isn't it?" Beron laughed. "You are not becoming missish again, are you, my love?"

She did not answer but he heard her breathing quicken. "Well," he said, "I suppose that you are quite right. A lady should not be required to disclose her feelings till she had received a proper declaration."

"Wh-what are you doing?" Deborah finally found her voice.

"I am agreeing," Beron explained as he dropped to one knee, "or rather I am complying with the manner in which you wish me to propose. I should, I admit, have foreseen your desire to manage this, as all else."

"I didn't...I mean I wasn't...I..."

"Pray observe, my love, that it is my left, my undamaged leg, that I am bending." He looked quizzically up at her. "I must hope that you will occasionally permit me to make some of my own decisions; after we are married, that is."

"You are absurd, sir." Deborah tried to speak casually, but she kept her eyes fixed on his face.

"At times," he acknowledged, "but not now, I promise you." He reached out a hand. "I love you dearly, Deborah, and I ask that you will do me the very great honour of becoming my wife."

Deborah clutched his hand. "But you can't wish to marry me! You can't! You think I'm meddlesome and interfering and—"

"Wholly adorable." In one swift movement, Lord Crichton rose and pulled Deborah into his arms. Before she could protest, he kissed her.

Much to her own surprise, Miss Stormont kissed him back.

The Duchesse whickered softly and shook her long ears. She regarded them with an expression as closely approximating approval as her aristocratic features would permit.

Both Miss Stormont and Lord Crichton ignored her. At last Deborah leaned a little way out of his arms, the better to see how the moonlight outlined the planes of his face. "Are you quite sure you wish to marry me?"

"I have wanted to marry you for a very long time. It unfortunately took me even longer to acknowledge it. I am, as I'm afraid you will discover, a most stubborn man."

She lifted a hand to touch his cheek, but he took it and raised it to his lips. "You have the most beautiful hands. I look forward to finding the most splendid ruby in Europe for them.''

Deborah sighed. ''I thought you had taken me in dislike and that I could never change your mind.''

''I have never disliked you. I hated the idea that you would disrupt my orderly, predictable and—'' he kissed the tip of her nose ''—very boring life. But now,'' he said, holding her tighter, ''I cannot imagine going back to that life.''

She sighed again in deepest satisfaction. ''When I was on the boat, I had a kind of premonition that everything was going to change. But I never dreamed that it would be so wonderful!''

''Didn't you, my love?'' He looked intensely into her dark eyes. ''And are you now quite sure that this is what you want? Do you truly wish to marry me?''

''Oh, yes!'' Miss Stormont's arms crept round his neck again. ''But you know I have never been used to go about in Society. I hope I shall not put you to the blush.''

''You could never do so.'' Beron's mouth curved mischievously. ''But I trust that you do not envision a life of unbridled Town gaiety? I hope you will like my country house just as much as I do and—'' his grip tightened ''—it has a most capacious nursery. I should very much like to spend a long time there, getting to know my new wife. And how will you like that, my dearest Debs?''

Miss Stormont raised her head and drew that generous mouth closer to her own. She whispered, ''I'll manage, my love, I'll manage.''

HISTORICAL

Bring back heartwarming memories of Christmas past,
with Historical Christmas Stories 1991, a collection of
romantic stories by three popular authors:

Christmas Yet To Come
by Lynda Trent

A Season of Joy
by Caryn Cameron

Fortune's Gift
by DeLoras Scott

A perfect Christmas gift!

H A R L E Q U I N

A Calendar of Romance

Be a part of American Romance's year-long celebration of love and the holidays of 1992. Experience all the passion of falling in love during the excitement of each month's holiday. Some of your favorite authors will help you celebrate those special times of the year, like the revelry of New Year's Eve, the romance of Valentine's Day, the magic of St. Patrick's Day.

Start counting down to the new year with

#421 HAPPY NEW YEAR, DARLING
by Margaret St. George

Read all the books in *A Calendar of Romance,* coming to you one each month, all year, from Harlequin American Romance.

American Romance®

Take 4 bestselling love stories FREE

Plus get a FREE surprise gift!

Special Limited-time Offer

Mail to Harlequin Reader Service®

In the U.S.	In Canada
3010 Walden Avenue	P.O. Box 609
P.O. Box 1867	Fort Erie, Ontario
Buffalo, N.Y. 14269-1867	L2A 5X3

YES! Please send me 4 free Harlequin Regency Romance® novels and my free surprise gift. Then send me 4 brand-new novels every month, and bill me at the low price of $2.69* each—a savings of 30¢ apiece off cover prices. There are no shipping, handling or other hidden costs. I understand that accepting the books and gift places me under no obligation ever to buy any books. I can always return a shipment and cancel at any time. Even if I never buy another book from Harlequin, the 4 free books and the surprise gift are mine to keep forever.

*Offer slightly different in Canada—$2.69 per book plus 49¢ per shipment for delivery. Canadian residents add applicable federal and provincial sales tax. Sales tax applicable in N.Y.

248 BPA ADL7   348 BPA ADMM

Name _____ (PLEASE PRINT)

Address _____ Apt. No. _____

City _____ State/Prov. _____ Zip/Postal Code _____

This offer is limited to one order per household and not valid to present Harlequin Regency Romance™ subscribers. Terms and prices are subject to change.

REG-91   © 1990 Harlequin Enterprises Limited

my VALENTINE 1992

Celebrate the most romantic day of the year with
MY VALENTINE 1992—a sexy new collection of four
romantic stories written by our famous Temptation
authors:

GINA WILKINS
KRISTINE ROLOFSON
JOANN ROSS
VICKI LEWIS THOMPSON

My Valentine 1992—an exquisite escape into a romantic
and sensuous world.

 Harlequin Books®

VAL-92-R